Demon in Lace

There was a thud overhead, that of a body falling and Beasley accepted the impossible.

"Shit," he swore and drew his gun.

"Kid, let's get out of here."

Beasley's revelation had come too late.

A woman came down the stairs behind Blauer. With a seemingly casual gesture she reached out, grabbed his head and twisted it. There was a crack and the rookie collapsed lifeless on the floor.

"The other one is upstairs in much the same condition," she said calmly as her gaze caught Beasley's. "You can hold a double funeral."

The detective knew he should do something — rush the woman, fire his pistol, run away — do *anything* but just stand there. But he couldn't. He was frozen, held by the woman's eyes as a rabbit in a spotlight.

Other titles from Bold Venture Press

A Name to Match My Soul
by James Bravewolf

Strictly Poison and Other Stories
by Charles Boeckman

The Plot Genie Index
by Wycliffe A. Hill

Plot Genie: Action Adventure
by Wycliffe A. Hill

The Jack Hagee series
by C.J. Henderson
No Free Lunch
Something For Nothing
Nothing Lasts Forever
No Torrent Like Greed
What You Pay For

Rich Harvey
Editor &
Cover Designer

"Blood is the Life" and "God's Work"
were originally published together as
"Death & Redemption" —
Flesh and Iron, Two Backed Books, 2007

A different version of "The Best Solution"
was originally published in
Crypt of Cthulhu, Vol 18, no 1, Hallowmas 1998.

ISBN-13: 978-1511568531
ISBN-10: w1511568534
Retail cover price: $9.95

Printed and bound in the United States.
10 9 8 7 6 5 4 3 2 1

Published by Bold Venture Press
www.boldventurepress.com

BLOOD
IS
THE LIFE

A "Bianca Jones" collection

John L. French

BOLD
VENTURE

"... for as to the life of all flesh, its blood is the life in it" (Leviticus 17:14)

"The blood is the life! The blood is the life!" (Bram Stoker, Dracula)

To my fellow monster hunters —
The men and women of the
Baltimore Police Crime Scene Unit

I.
Blood Is The Life

HE remembered the party, and the woman — tall, beautiful, exotic. She was every woman he had ever dreamt of and he knew from that night on he'd dream only of her.

She chose him. Out of all the men there she chose him. They talked for a while, neither saying anything important, and then she asked, "Is there somewhere we could go?"

"My place?" he offered in a weak voice full of hope. She nodded and they left with every male in the place wishing to be him.

He never made it home, not that night, not ever. "Let's go there," she suggested, looking across the street.

"The park?"

"Yes, the park, where it is dark and quiet. Where two people can be alone with nature and each other." She pressed tight against him and there was no question where they would end up.

Out of sight of the house, beyond the view of any-one else. "This looks like a good place."

"Yes." Leaning against a tree, she pulled him to her.

They kissed, his tongue in her mouth then hers in his. His hand ran up her leg and under her skirt, caressing her through her panties. Her hand dropped between them. Finding him hard, she squeezed tight.

Her other hand pushed him back.

"What?"

"Shhh!" She unzipped him, unbuckled his belt, took out his erection. He moved his hands so as to pull down her panties.

"Not yet." She kissed him again, gently this time, her lips barely touching his before moving across his cheek and down to his neck. She started stroking him, slowly at first, then faster.

"You should stop." She ignored him. "If you don't stop I'm going to …"

"Yes, I know." She bit deep into his neck.

He screamed, more from surprise then pain, then relaxed. He'd been marked before, and had worn the love bite as a badge of honor. But then his blood flowed and she began to drink.

An ancient part of him realized what was happen-ing and tried to send a warning. "Push her off, run away, flee now." But he could not help surrendering to the feelings of peace and pleasure that washed over him.

He spurted into her hand and her lips left his neck just long enough to lick her fingers. I should stop, she thought, and leave him alive with a few pleasant memories. But she was hungry and excited. Again her teeth found his neck and his life faded away as she drank deep.

When she was done she let the body drop to the ground. It had been some time since she had so completely drained a victim. There were things she should do, but not right yet. Just now she wanted to enjoy the afterglow of having fed. There would be time before dawn. She leaned back against the tree and closed her eyes ...

"Warren!" The shout woke her up. "Where are you, man?"

"I told you, Warren split with that hot Asian chick."

"Asian, she looked Indian to me."

"India's part of Asia, asshole. Whatever she was, Warren got lucky and left us."

"His car's still here."

"So they took hers. And since I know where he hides a spare key, we can take his. C'mon, the sun's almost up and the ex is dropping off the kid this morning. I gotta get a little sleep."

The sun was almost up, she realized. She had best get home. It would not be good to be out after dawn. An inner sense told her she had just enough time. She looked down at the body.

"There isn't time to care for you properly. Maybe you'll be one of the lucky ones, maybe not. But just in case." She rolled the body into a shallow ditch and quickly covered it with twigs and leaves.

***

HE WOKE to the hunger, his need less an appetite than a dagger in his soul, a pain that would not abate until he fed. Slowly, he pushed aside the leafy branches that were his covers and crawled out of the shallow dirt pit that was his bed.

Night came late that time of year. He did not have much time to hunt. Fortunately, he was not the only one who haunted the park. There were always men and women who used the darkness as a blanket to cover their own activities. Lovers who had nowhere else to go, users and dealers who bought and sold, people who wished to hide things so that they'd never be found — all had their reasons for being in the park. He only had to find one, then he could rest and forget until he woke again.

He hated his life — no, what he had was not life, merely existence. Wake, feed, and sleep; that's all that was left to him since the party. How long ago was that? A week? Two weeks? Three? He could not remember. He did remember the woman and how he had awakened in the ditch that was now his home, with hunger gnawing at him and a newly born instinct of how to satisfy it.

He tried to end it, the morning after his first kill. The feeding had been savage and messy and filled him with disgust and self-loathing. The thought of his victim lying bloody on the path drove him to find a clearing and wait for the sun and its deadly cleansing rays.

As expected, he burned, and burned, and burned.

But he didn't die and fall to ash as he hoped he would. When the pain grew too great he sought the darkness of the woods. Later he tried a gun and then a knife, both taken from his kills. Neither worked. Using the knife he sharpened a stake, but remembering how the sun had failed him, he did not have the courage to use it. So he slept and woke and hunted. But most of all he waited. There could only be one end and he prayed it would come soon.

***

THE news quickly spread through police headquarters, Bianca Jones was back. Everyone knew that the detective had been suspended several weeks ago over a shooting incident in Federal Hill, but no one knew the circumstances. One story had her hunting down and executing a serial rapist. Another that she'd been ambushed by a drug gang. A third said that she'd rescued a woman taken hostage by an escaped killer. Then there were rumors about a cult in Pennsylvania.

None of the stories were true. Few people knew what really happened. They were sworn to secrecy and the truth was such that none of them wanted to think about it, much less talk about it. Not that anyone would have believed them.

Major Chester Williams was one of the select few. After long and heated discussions, he finally convinced the top brass of the Baltimore Police to bring Bianca back from exile.

"Please sit down, Detective Jones," Williams said

when Bianca came into his office. He held up two file folders containing Bianca's accounts of the incidents in Pennsylvania and Federal Hill. "Two very interesting reports, detective, if they're the truth. A creature from another dimension abducting and impregnating women on Federal Hill. After that, a wannabe coven manages to call up yet another creature. And you somehow manage to stop both monsters all by yourself."

Bianca did not think it wise to mention Morgan, who was so much more than the Fells Point bookseller he seemed to be. Morgan was the one who had enlisted her in the war against the forces of evil, a war whose battleground now seemed to be centered on Baltimore.

"That's what happened, sir. Joe Russo has forensic evidence that backs me up and ..."

"I believe you."

This simple sentence was said with such sincerity that Bianca shut up and just stared at Williams. She hadn't expected anyone outside those involved to accept the truth. Maybe she wouldn't lose her job after all.

"Surprised, Detective? Then you'll be even more surprised to learn that you're not the first member of this department to have an encounter with the supernatural."

"I would, sir. I haven't heard of any."

Williams smiled. "You weren't supposed to. Baltimore's over two hundred years old. It's has its share of ghosts and other things unseen. Poe's death was due to more than drugs and alcohol. He played with the darkness and it finally caught up with him. Then there was the Great Fire of 1904. Those Carmelite nuns who turned the path of the blaze were praying for more than O'Neill's Dry Goods. And remember those headless fortune tellers from several years back?"

"I've heard about them."

"What you heard were lies. There was more to that case than a crazy man who didn't like the color of their candles."

Williams got up from his desk and walked over to a large shredder in the corner of his office. He began feeding Bianca's reports into it. "Federal Hill never happened. Pennsylvania never happened. There were no monsters, just a cult you were investigating and finally put an end to."

"That's the official version?"

"That's the only version as far as the public and most of the department is concerned." Williams waited for Bianca's reaction. She nodded her agreement.

"So where does that leave me?"

"Your suspension is lifted. Technically, since you were supposed to be tracking this cult, it never existed, so you'll be reinstated with back pay. And you have a new assignment, if you want it."

Without having to ask, Bianca knew what the job was. "Monster hunter."

Williams nodded. "Something like that. You'd be assigned to Special Investigations, routine work mostly — undercover, stake outs, surveillance, cases of a sensitive or political nature. But if something out of the ordinary comes up, it's yours to handle however you have to."

When she joined the department, Bianca had taken an oath to protect Baltimore against those who would do its citizens harm. Thieves, murderers, drug dealers, rapists — she'd been hunting monsters all along but at least they'd been human. The things that dwelt in the darkness saw humanity as cattle to be herded, obstacles to their dominion, nuisances to be wiped out. They were literally the stuff of nightmares, her nightmares to be exact. Bianca had had many restless nights of late, with unnamable things haunting her dreams.

Could she keep doing it, she asked herself. Risking her life was one thing, that came with the job. But could she keep rolling the dice with her sanity and maybe her soul as the stakes?

Sensing her hesitation, Williams said, "There's no one else who can do the job."

And that was the hell of it. There was no one else in the department who had faced creatures from beyond, spit in their many eyes and sent them back to the Abyss. She'd done the job twice now and lived to tell about it. Bianca had no choice but to accept.

"Glad to hear it. Here's your first case."

***

AFTER settling in her office, Bianca went down to the Crime Lab to see Joe Russo, both to let the criminalist know she'd been reinstated and to ask him a favor.

"Bianca! Welcome back!" Joe greeted her from his workbench.

"Good to be back, Joe. I wanted to stop by and thank you for your help in the Federal Hill case."

"I wish I could have done more."

"You did more than anyone else, and I haven't forgotten that I owe you a dinner."

The look on Joe's face told Bianca that he hadn't forgotten either, and was looking forward to it. So was she, she realized with some surprise.

"Joe, if you have time after work, can you meet me at Morgan's? There are some things we have to discuss."

***

LIKE all good bookstores, Morgan's Rare Books and Collectibles was crowded, not with customers, but with volumes and volumes of books filling the shelves, stacked on the floors and occupying every available vertical space except for a few strategically placed chairs.

After letting himself in through the front door, Joe looked around for Bianca. There was no sign of her. In fact, except for himself, there didn't seem to anyone in the store. He was just about to call out when ...

"Can I help you?"

The voice that seemingly came from nowhere was dry and thin, an old man's voice. The old man it belonged to stepped out from behind the bookcase that had hidden him. He was a small man, no bigger than Bianca's five feet. But despite his age and wizened appearance Joe sensed a strength about him.

"Can I help you?" the man asked again.

"Mr. Morgan?"

"Just Morgan, young man, and you are?"

"Joe, Joe Russo."

"You're Miss Jones's friend, aren't you?" Morgan said, shaking the hand that Joe had offered. "The one that helped us with that unpleasantness in Federal Hill."

"Uh, yes," Joe admitted, strangely pleased that Bianca had mentioned him to this man. "Although I don't know how much help I was."

"More than you think. Now I'm guessing that you're not here to see me or even buy a book. You're here to see Miss Jones." Before Joe could answer Morgan added, "She's not here."

"I know, she asked me to meet her here."

The bookseller's eyebrows rose, "Is something happening that I should know about?"

"Probably, but as to what ..." Joe shrugged his shoulders.

"Very well, let's wait for Miss Jones. And while we're waiting, browse around. You just might find a book or two that will look better on your shelf than mine."

The front room of the shop was much like any other used bookstore Joe had visited, bookcases and shelves running along the walls with more set at right angles to them, the arrangement forming small cubicles for each subject matter. Joe skipped over history, social sciences and the like and headed right for popular fiction.

While Morgan had a good selection of horror, science fiction and fantasy, Joe was disappointed to find little in the way of mystery. "I leave that for Kathy up the street," Morgan explained in passing, referring to the mystery bookstore a bit north on Fleet St.

"Any true crime?" Joe asked.

"Some, it's mostly up front ... you're with the Crime Lab, aren't you?"

"Yes, inside mostly, but I still do crime scenes sometimes."

"Then come with me."

As Morgan led him into the back of the store, Joe couldn't help but notice that the inside of the shop was larger than the outside suggested. Wasn't this store in the rear of another? Then why was there a back door? Before he could ask, the old man put a heavy volume in his hands.

The book was without dustjacket, and seemed to be as old as its owner. Joe looked at the title embossed on front. *The Whole Art of Detection.* Could it be? There was no author credit on front. Joe opened to the title page, saw the name he expected. Below the name was the simple signature "Sigerson."

"His idea of a joke," Morgan commented. "As far as I know, he never signed his own name to one."

The two were still admiring the book when Bianca walked in. Nodding a greeting she got right to business.

"Morgan, what do you know about vampires?"

Both men stared at her. Morgan with a detached kind of interest, Joe with a jaw-dropped gaze of disbelief.

"You're kidding, right?"

"I wish I was, Joe. And it may yet be a false alarm, but sit down and I'll tell you both about it."

Bianca took a BPD case folder out of the brief case she was carrying. "Four bodies, all found in Druid Hill Park," she read from the report. "Their throats were ripped out."

Joe nodded. "I've heard about these but haven't worked on any. Word is Homicide first thought that it was some wild animal that escaped from the Maryland Zoo. But all their beasts are present and accounted for. After the second body they started looking for a nut job. The Animal Shelter's been called just in case."

"What you haven't heard was the cause of death. The Medical Examiner was asked to keep that quiet. All four died of extreme exsanguination. Less than a pint of blood left in any of them, and yet ..." Bianca took some crime scene photos from the folder. "There's no blood on any of the scenes."

"So the victims were killed elsewhere and dumped in the park."

Ignoring Joe's suggestion, Bianca handed the photos to Morgan. "What do you think?"

"A vampire," the bookseller declared after studying the photographs. "And seemingly a young one."

"A child?"

"No, Miss Jones. By child I meant one new to the life, so to speak. From these photographs, and what you've told me, this one gorges, draining his victims dry, then sleeps for five or six days before having to hunt again. As he gets older ..."

"If he gets older," Bianca interrupted.

"Yes, if he gets older, he will need less blood, and should learn to pace himself."

"What about his victims?"

"His victims, Mr. Russo?"

"Yeah, if our killer is a vampire, why haven't his victims crawled out of the grave and started biting people?"

"Depending on the vampire, that is not always the case. And even if it were, the procedures that a body endures during autopsy and embalming pretty much guarantee that it will not rise again."

"You said, 'depending on the vampire.' Are there different kinds?"

"Several, Miss Jones, and the most dangerous will take not just your blood but your very soul."

Bianca took the photos back from Morgan and replaced them in the case folder. "Let's hope this one is just a regular bloodsucker."

"It is," Morgan confirmed.

"So what can kill it?"

"Decapitation. Modern weapons will slow him down, but not necessarily destroy him. A vampire will die if exposed to direct sunlight, although in today's' world there is so much smog and pollution that that would be a very long and painful death."

"What about crosses, garlic and stuff like that?" Joe asked.

"Garlic, Mr. Russo, is only effective in the kitchen. And religious items have only the power you, or rather, your belief gives them. If you truly believe in the power of God, however you know Him, then a cross can be effective protection. If, however, you are an unbeliever, is it merely two pieces of wood."

"Unless the vampire believes in it."

"There is that, Miss Jones. A new-born would have been conditioned to fear religious items by movies and books. But I would think your main problem would be finding the creature."

"Don't worry about that, Morgan. Just tell me what I'm facing when I do find him."

"Vampires are by their nature stronger than humans. He'll be even stronger at night and after he's fed. But even in the daytime he can still be dangerous, especially if he's not directly in the sun."

"Like if he was shaded by trees or something."

"Precisely, Mr. Russo. Miss Jones, when you do go after this creature, take as much protection and firepower as you can. And if you are a believer, Mass and Communion on the morning of the hunt would not be remiss."

***

"Why me?" Joe wanted to know.

After conferring with Morgan, Bianca and Joe stopped at the Blue Moon Café for a late dinner.

"Because Morgan wasn't hungry."

"No, I mean, why bring me into all this? I'm not up on this supernatural stuff; I'm just a crime lab tech."

"You're more than that, Joe. You're a friend I can trust to be there when needed."

"A friend?" He gave a questioning look.

"Let's start there and see what happens."

"Fair enough." After a few minutes Joe added, "There has to be some other explanation."

"To being friends?"

"To the idea of the undead in Baltimore."

"There are probably several, Joe, and Homicide is checking on all of them. In the meantime, Williams wants his personal Ghostbuster to go one step beyond. And just in case ..."

Bianca took a chain from her blouse. At its end was a gold cross. "And tonight I'm going to sharpen some stakes and order silver bullets from the Internet."

Joe looked across the table at Bianca. "How do you do it?"

"There's a Lone Ranger website that ..."

"No, I mean this, this monster thing. I've only know what I've read and what you've told me and I'm more than a little freaked. You've seen them, fought them and it doesn't seem to bother you. And now you're talking about going after a vampire like he's just another criminal."

"Because, Joe, to me that's all he is. I was in the Sex Crimes Unit. There I saw it all — abuse, rape, torture. Women brutalized, children bought and sold as playthings, sexual predators stalking the elderly. I've been fighting monsters for the past five years. The only difference now is that the perps aren't human."

"The stakes are higher."

Bianca shrugged. "Just life and death, Joe; the way it's always been."

***

SHE was running through a dark forest, chased by the blood-maddened undead. Fanged bats flew about her head, herding her towards the sound of hungry wolves. The stake she carried was splintered and her cross broken in two. Nowhere to run, no way to fight, and surrender was not an option. She looked around for anything she could use as a weapon. She found nothing. As the horrors drew closer, she realized there was another way. She could ...

Somewhere between the middle of the night and early in the morning, Bianca woke with a start. Alone in her apartment, she realized that while she could lie to Joe and most of the time to herself, the truth came out in dreams. It was more than life and death, it was life after death and death after life. If she fought this creature — win or lose — she herself could be infected, become the thing she'd sworn to destroy. And that's what scared her most. It was not just this case. That was the risk she'd be taking from now on, that was her challenge — to stand in the light, to fight the darkness and not stray too far into the shadows.

Morning came. Despite her fears of the previous night, Bianca still had a job to do. There was a killer to be caught, a bloodsucker to be staked. Remembering all of Morgan's precautions, she made herself ready for the hunt.

***

THEY met in the park. When Joe pulled up in the Crime Lab van, he saw four uniformed officers standing by the Quick Response Team truck. They were carrying shotguns and wearing helmets and body armor. Bianca was talking to three people in civilian clothes, all with dogs on leads. "You understand what you're to do?" she asked them.

One of them, a woman with a dachshund, spoke for the group. "You're looking for a dead body. If we find it, we tell you where it is and leave."

A man with a black Labrador was looking nervously at the heavily armed men. "Is this dangerous?"

Bianca gave the group the smile that all police officers give to civilians to whom they're about to lie. "Not at all. Just a precaution. It's required whenever civilian personnel are involved." Or when you're hunting the undead, she thought. "Now please get your partners ready while I talk to the officers."

Joe caught up with her. "Been to church lately?"

"This morning. Took Communion just as Morgan suggested. You?"

"Said a few prayers, mostly for you. So what gives with the kennel club?"

"They're cadaver dogs, Joe. They're trained to hunt for dead bodies in the wake of major disasters. What better way to find a vampire?"

"And what do you want me to do?"

"Just a minute." The pair had reached the QRT officers. "Good morning, gentlemen, thank you for coming out."

"How can we help you, Detective?"

Feeling the eyes of all four men looking down on her, Bianca gave them their orders. "We're after a real nutcase this time, the man we think has been doing the park murders. This asshole thinks he's a vampire, and he may have partly buried himself somewhere around here. That's what the dogs are for. If they find him, I'll approach him alone so as not to set him off. I should be able to handle him."

Sergeant Tavon Greggs was in command of the Response Team. "And if you're not?"

"If I'm not, Sergeant, if I go down and he gets by me, you and your men are to stop him using deadly force."

"Deadly force? Are you sure, Detective?"

Bianca handed him an envelope. "Here is your authorization from Major Williams, Sergeant. The man we're after kills people with just his hands and teeth. He is an extreme danger to the public. He is not to escape the park. He gets one chance, with me. After that, take him down hard — head and body shots and keep firing until he stops twitching or he's nothing but little bits of flesh."

Greggs looked at his men, to make sure they had all heard her orders. Then he looked back at Bianca. He'd heard the stories and rumors about her and hadn't believed any of them — until now.

"As you say, Detective. You got that, men? Give the detective her shot. If the suspect gets by her, go Rambo on his ass."

With QRT standing ready, and the dogs straining on their leads, Bianca walked over to Joe.

"You asked me to come out here, Bianca. What's my job?"

"Right now, just stand by — stay in the background and out of the line of fire. I'll need you once I take this thing down."

"And if you don't?"

"If QRT starts firing, get the hell out of here. Tell Morgan what happened. He'll know what to do and who to call."

"What about you?"

"I'll be past worrying about." I hope, Bianca added silently. "But let's think positive."

She got a bag out of her car. On her signal, the dog handlers released their partners. With baying and barking, the freed dogs sniffed the air, looking for a scent. Finding something, they ran off into the woods.

***

HE FELT the sun's rays through his covering of leaves and branches and an inner sense told him that it had been up for three hours. For the first time since his change he had awakened during the day. He didn't know why. He had killed only a few nights ago and his appetite, while always present, was not demanding that he rise and feed. Suddenly, a newly developed instinct told him why he had shaken off his sleep and the knowledge was as sure as his need for blood.

They were coming for him.

Relief flooded his mind. Finally it was to be over. No longer would he be driven to hunt and kill, no longer would he need blood to sustain his pitiful existence. Those who hunted him would know what to do. They would succeed where he had failed and deliver him to a peaceful rest.

Or would they? He had killed. Though he had been driven to it by uncontrollable need and desire, it was his teeth that had ripped out throats, his mouth on the open wounds and his throat down which the warm sweet blood had flowed. Once truly dead, would his judgment be based on how he lived his life before that night in the park or on what he had done afterwards? Had his surrender to the lust for blood also condemned his soul? And if it had, could God's Hell be any worse than the one he was living in now?

Primal urges seized him. Why take the chance? Why not fight those coming after him, kill them, drink their blood then flee deeper into the woods. Wasn't each feeding sweeter than the last? And the next would be sweeter still. Imagine how it would be in a year. Sharp fangs biting into warn flesh and the ecstasy of drinking life-giving blood better than the feel of any woman.

Passion, fear, disgust and despair all warred inside him. And as he felt the hunt come closer and heard the barking of hounds draw nearer, he waited and wondered what he would do when he was uncovered.

***

THE dogs were close. Bianca could tell by how quick they were now to return to their human partners and signal them to follow. Soon she heard the woman with the dachshund cry out, "Found something!"

With the QRT officers following at a distance behind her, Bianca caught up with the search team about hundred yards off the main path. The woods there were thick, the sunlight barely penetrating through the trees. All three dogs were circling a loose mound of branches and leaves, none of them coming too close to it. "Looks like someone just threw him in there and covered him over," said man with the Labrador.

This was it, Bianca was certain of it. She dismissed the team. "Thank you all, you can go now."

"Don't you want us to stay until you're sure?"

"Go. Now." Bianca ordered in a tone that was not to be disobeyed. The three left with their dogs.

Their departure was the signal for the QRT officers to stand ready. They circled Bianca's position, far back out of sight as ordered, but ready to move in and inflict lethal damage at her cry or command.

Bianca opened her bag, took out a crucifix and hung it around her neck. Then she removed a sharpened stake. After uttering a silent prayer, Bianca started removing the branches from the mound.

***

As HIS grave was uncovered all he saw and felt was light. There were the rays of the sun, even filtered as they were they still burned. But there were brighter lights coming from the woman. Lights that both warmed and repulsed him, lights that he shrank from yet wanted to embrace. One hung around her neck and the other shone from inside her. The beast within wanted to tear the woman into pieces, eat her flesh, drink her blood. Anything to destroy the lights.

"No," that which was still human in him cried out.

Whatever the consequences, it was time to end this, to surrender to the lights and accept whatever was to come. The stake came toward him and gladly he rose to meet it.

***

It was over faster than she'd thought. The vampire came up, an accepting look in his dead eyes. He made no effort to avoid the stake that Bianca plunged into his heart. He fell back into the grave, his rictus grin looking oddly peaceful.

That was easy, Bianca thought. She looked down at the corpse and waited for the rapid decay she was sure would start. It didn't. Damn, she silently cursed. I was counting on that. Now how am I going to explain having shoved a stake through a suspect's heart?

"Detective, are you okay?" Bianca heard Sergeant Greggs call.

Well, here goes.

"All clear," she replied and within seconds the armed men were with her and staring down at the dead man.

"Jesus, did you do that?"

"Don't be an ass, Donaldson," the sergeant said. "Look at that thing; it's been dead for at least two days. No way Detective Jones did that."

He turned to Bianca. Whatever he thought, whatever he suspected, he was keeping it to himself. "Not that anyone would have been too upset if you had. Just a damn shame someone had to beat you to it. Anyway, we'll secure now, Ma'am. On our way out we'll tell that crime lab guy you need him. Should I call Homicide for you?"

"Thanks, Sergeant, but I can take care of everything else."

Greggs looked back at the body. "I'm sure you can, Detective. I'm sure you can."

***

"So WHERE is the vampire now?"

"He's in the back of my van."

After the Quick Response Team had left the park, Joe and Bianca had wrapped the undead corpse in a body bag and driven straight to Morgan's store.

Morgan nodded his approval. "Good, he will need to be destroyed."

"I thought Bianca did that when she staked him."

"No, Mr. Russo, she did not. The stake merely incapacitates the beast."

"That explains why the body hasn't started decomposing."

"Correct, Miss Jones. The decay that sergeant noted was from the period of his death and revival. To truly destroy the vampire we must decapitate or burn it."

"You mean that body in the back of my van isn't dead yet?" The silence from Morgan and Bianca was his answer. "And we're going to kill it?"

Bianca looked at her friend and saw the pain and confusion in his face. "That's my job, Joe. It's what I do. Find monsters and destroy them."

"But you don't always destroy them, do you,

Bianca?" Joe stood up, began pacing around the bookstore's back room. "You told me about the book locked up in Morgan's safe. In it is a whole world of monsters you refuse to destroy."

"That's different, Joe."

"How? You locked the book up, why can't we just lock the thing up?"

"The book is safe where it is, Mr. Russo. But there is no sure way of confining a vampire. Should he escape, more will die."

"I know, I know, but out in my van in a living, breathing creature. Well, living anyway. I just can't accept that we're calmly sitting around drinking tea and planning to execute it."

Morgan gestured for Joe to sit down. Once the crime lab tech was beside him, the bookseller took hold of his arm and looked at him. For a minute that was all he did, stared into Joe's eyes, searching for and finding the innocence that was inside the young man. Then he opened his own self to Joe, letting him see the painful decisions he'd had to make, the horrible things he'd had to do in his fight against dark things.

"It is not easy," Morgan finally said, hoping that Joe would understand, "to deliberately plan the death of what was once as human as you or I. It leaves a mark on one's soul that nothing can erase. It is a price we willingly pay, in this world and the next, to keep our world safe. I wish it were otherwise, but there is nothing else to do."

As Bianca had listened quietly to first Joe's complaint and Morgan's answer, she found herself agreeing with both. She understood the concept of deadly force, had used it on occasion to save herself and others. Still, as much as she knew the vampire had to be destroyed, killing what seemed to be a helpless prisoner went against all she believed in. But she saw no other way. So she reviewed what little she knew about the undead — what they were, how they died, how they could be stopped.

"There's one thing we could try." As the two men turned toward her, she told them her idea, one that, even to her, was both blasphemous and incredible.

"We could go to Hell for even thinking this," Joe said, not quite willing to consider what Bianca had suggested.

Morgan thought for a moment. "It can't hurt to try, not us anyway. For the vampire it could be quite painful. And I think the Lord will forgive us our presumption if we fail."

"Then let's do it. Joe, do you want out?"

The crime lab man shook his head. "Where you go, I go, wherever it leads."

Bianca rewarded Joe with a smile then asked Morgan, "Know a friendly priest?"

***

THERE was blackness all around him. It wasn't the dark of the grave or the sweet forgetfulness of sleep. He knew them both well. This was more like oblivion, the sense that beyond himself there was nothing. And if that were all, if there was only unending blackness, he could have accepted it. But there was also the pain.

The pain was his whole world, taking away even his thirst. It was the one thing besides himself that existed in the blackness. It centered in his chest and radiated in all directions, extending to the tips of his toes and fingers. It was fire and ice, sharp needles and blunt trauma. It was unending and he knew himself to be in Hell. Had he a voice he would have screamed and had he not thought himself already damned he would have prayed for deliverance.

After an eternity of suffering there came a voice in the distance and with the voice a light that banished some of the pain. He knew the light despite having seen it only once before, just before the stake had condemned him.

"I'm told you can hear me," said the voice. "I hope so. I'm going to remove the stake. If you want to live, stay very still. If you move at all the stake goes back and that will be the end of you."

The voice offered salvation. He waited and soon the pressure in his chest was relieved and the pain and blackness went away. He looked up to see a woman standing above him, a bloody stake, his bloody stake, in one hand and a shining light in her other. He wanted to run from the light but remembering her words stayed where he was.

His vision cleared. He was in what looked like a cellar. The woman stood waiting above him. Beyond her was an old man with a shotgun, both barrels trained on him. Slowly, deliberately, he spoke his first words in several weeks.

"I want to live."

The woman nodded. A liquid-filled bag flew at him, landed on his chest. Even through the plastic he could smell the rich blood inside.

"Drink," the woman ordered, "then we'll talk."

***

BIANCA watched the vampire drink down the pint of blood she'd gotten from a friend at City of Hope Hospital. Like a kid with a sip-pack she thought. And he wasn't that far from being a kid. In the light of the bookshop's basement, her prisoner looked less like an undead monster and more like a runaway who'd been on the streets too long. Looking past the dirt and decay, she doubted if he were old enough to legally drink wine.

She waited until he finished, suppressing her disgust as he licked his lips and fingers clean then tore open the plastic and did the same to the inside of the bag.

Bianca waited until he was done. "The shotgun behind me fires silver pellets. If you move, you're dead."

"I understand," the young man said calmly, averting his eyes from the crucifix she kept between them.

"Good. What's your name?"

"Warren Trent," he said after a moment.

"What happened to you, Warren?"

He had relived that moment so many times that the story came easier to him than his own name. He told Bianca about the after-hours party, the woman and about what he'd done after he woke up.

"Two choices, Warren. The first is that stake goes back. We behead you, burn your body and scatter your ashes. You die unmourned and without making payment for those you killed."

"What's my other choice?"

When Bianca told him he was amazed at its simplicity. He quickly agreed. Anything, he thought, to avoid the darkness brought by the stake and, he was surprised to realize, for the chance to make things right.

Moran lowered the shotgun as Joe Russo came down the basement stairs accompanied by a middle-aged man wearing a clerical collar.

"Father Lawrence, good to see you again."

"I wish I could say the same, Morgan. The archbishop tells me you're causing trouble again."

"This time I'm doing your job, trying to save a soul. The young man who met you at the door is Joe Russo and the young lady with the cross is Bianca Jones. Both are with the Baltimore Police. This young man," Morgan gestured with shotgun, "is Warren Trent. He's a vampire and would like to take Communion."

Father Anton Lawrence was an inquisitor for the Vatican's Holy Order, one of the few in North America and the only one in the northeast. As such, he had confronted demons, cast out devils and destroyed satanic cults. He had seen much in his thirty years in the service of God. But after he heard Morgan's request and had suppressed the anger that rose up in him, all he could say was, "I don't believe it."

"Believe it, Father. He's a vampire."

The priest was barley keeping his rage in check. "Young lady, I believe that's he's a vampire. I just don't believe that you expect me to offer the Lord's Body and Blood to such an unholy creature. It would be a ..."

"Sacrilege?" All eyes turned to Trent, who was still sitting on the floor, held there more by the force of Bianca's crucifix than the threat of Morgan's gun. Moving slowly so that nothing he did would be mistaken as a threat, he stood and faced the priest.

"If I'm already damned maybe it is a sacrilege. But can the damned hope for salvation, or for mercy?"

"How far does the Lord's Mercy extend, Anton? Are you the one to set limits on it?"

Father Lawrence considered Morgan's words. Then he thought of the words of consecration and as he did his anger subsided. He turned toward Trent.

"It won't be easy."

Addressed by the priest, the vampire felt the same repulsion he did from the cross. Fighting it the best he could, he replied, "I understand."

"And it may be painful."

Trent thought of sunlight and the stake. "I expect it will be."

"And it will take great faith, on all our parts. Do you believe that this will work, Mr. Trent?"

"I pray it will, Father."

"I do believe, help my unbelief," Bianca quoted.

"Then let us begin. And I ask you all, as a sign of your faith, to put down your weapons."

Father Lawrence looked at Morgan, then to Bianca. At their hesitation he said, "If you don't believe in this man, why should I?" The crucifix and shotgun were lowered to floor, both still within arm's reach. The priest shook his head.

"Oh ye of little faith." Pointing to Joe, he said, "Take these things, the stake too, and put them in the corner, then bring that table over."

As Joe complied, Father Lawrence moved slightly, giving Trent a clear path to the door and waited to see what the now unrestrained vampire would do. When Trent remained still, he smiled. "This might just work. Let us begin."

From the bag he had brought with him, Father Lawrence set out on the table a gold paten and on them a few hosts. A small bottle of wine and a chalice followed. The priest began the ritual of consecration.

Trent barely heard the words. As the priest spoke the holy words there came a roaring in his ears and he felt the beast rise up once more. The fools, how easy it would be to slaughter them all. He saw it clearly in his mind. Moving quickly, he'd kill men outright, then turn on the woman. She was the one who used the stake on him, who caused him to suffer. She would die in anguish as he slowly drained her and maybe use her in other ways. No, not maybe, he'd use her every way he could.

The beast inside him was strong. Trent fought to contain it but it seemed a losing battle. Then the words of the priest came through.

"...He took the cup. Again He gave You thanks and praise, gave the cup to His disciples, and said 'This is the cup of my blood, the blood of the new and everlasting covenant. It will be shed for you and for all so that sins may be forgiven.'"

And the air was filled with the scent of warm blood.

Trent watched the priest take one of the hosts for himself then offer the others to the two men and the woman. The old man declined, the others accepted. The priest took a sip from the chalice, then turned toward him.

"Warren, this is the Blood of Christ. Take and drink, for it is life eternal."

Trent took the chalice from the priest's hands, his fingers burning where they touched the cup. Accepting the pain, he held the cup even tighter and brought its rim to his lips. The beast made one final effort and urged him to throw the wine in the priest's face, take his vengeance and make his escape. But Trent caught the sweet scent of wine and blood and drank deep.

The liquid was fire going down his throat, a fire that quickly spread throughout his body. Trent had thought that there could nothing worse than the pain of the stake.

He was wrong.

***

"I THINK we killed him."

"I think you're right, Bianca."

"Then we failed."

"Not exactly, young lady."

Father Lawrence pointed to the body of Warren Trent, still lying where it had fallen after the taking of

Communion. The two days of decay it had suffered was slowly fading, to be replaced with unmarred skin.

"Thanks to you he died in Christ and that is a blessing. You've all done well today."

Bianca didn't see it as a victory. True, she'd wanted to heal this man, to break the curse he was under, both for his own sake and that of the law she served. Trent was a killer several times over, his victims dying horrible deaths, and she'd wanted to see him pay, either jail in this life or punishment in the next. Now the priest was telling her that Trent had been redeemed. As a Catholic she knew she should be glad, but as a cop she felt cheated.

"Let's bag him up, Joe," she said as Morgan led Father Lawrence from the basement. "He's late for the morgue."

***

Two days later Joe sought Bianca out in her office. "Guess where I've been?"

She didn't have to guess, the smudge of fingerprint powder on his left cheek was a giveaway. "Out on a burglary."

"Yes, but where?"

Bianca shook her head. "Tell me and we'll both know."

"The Medical Examiner's Office. Last night someone broke in and stole a body. And for the bonus question, guess whose?"

Again she didn't have to guess. The memory of what had happened in Morgan's basement was still fresh in her mind. Bianca sat back in her chair. "Shit, it was Trent's, wasn't it?"

Joe answered in the worse Bela Lugosi Bianca had ever heard, "Dracula has risen from the dead." Then added in his normal voice, "We going after him?"

Bianca thought for a moment then shook her head. "The priest said he's been redeemed. I'm going to go with that. If he starts up again I'll find him, stake him and throw him in the Chesapeake Bay. Let the crabs have him. Until then, it's business as usual. Williams has me on stake out duty tonight. We still on for dinner Friday night?"

"Wouldn't miss it. After all, you're buying."

***

FOR the second time Warren Trent woke from the sleep of death. This time there was no hunger, no pain. The fire of the Blood had cleansed him. From inside his body bag he worked the zipper open and slowly slid off the gurney that was his bed. Feeling his way in the darkness he found the door of the cold storage room and opened it, hoping there was no one on the other side.

There wasn't. It was night and the morgue was deserted, occupied only by him and bodies shrouded in white plastic. He looked down and saw that he was naked and felt ashamed. He looked around a locker room until he found clothing that fit. And then, renewed and reborn, he walked out into the night and a new life.   ♦

II.
God's Work

H E had lives to pay for — his own life for one, but mostly the lives of the people he had killed before he had been given his second chance. Dead, he had been restored to life. Damned, he had been redeemed. A creature of darkness, Warren Trent now walked in the light.

There had been a party; he had gone off with a woman. No, not a woman but a creature of darkness in the guise of one. She used him and left him for dead or worse. He arose, condemned to hunt the night for victims for whose blood he needed to survive.

After terrorizing the city for over a month, Trent was tracked down and staked, the stake sending him to a hellish oblivion from which he could find no escape. And then he was offered a chance at salvation.

The woman who had stopped him, a police detective named Bianca Jones, gave him a choice. He could die the final death — alone, unmourned and unforgiven — or he could seek forgiveness by taking

Communion, drinking wine transformed to the Blood of Christ. Trent chose the latter, died and was reborn yet again.

With his redemption had come a sense of purpose. He had been saved, now it was his duty to seek out others who had fallen and lead them to salvation. He walked out of the morgue resolved to leave Baltimore, search the country seeking out the undead and preach to them the Gospel of the Blood of Life. Everyone he saved would be a small repayment on the debt he owed.

Finding the undead was easy. Trent discovered that as a result of his previous affliction he had an affinity for others like he had been. It wasn't that he was drawn to them, just that he was aware of a vampire's presence whenever one was near. And the others were aware of him.

He learned this in Philadelphia. He was drinking in a small bar off Broad St. when he felt — something. He wasn't sure just how, but he suddenly knew that in a roomful of strangers he was no longer alone.

The man who sat down next to him was short, fat and balding. But there was an aura about him that Trent recognized at once.

"You feel like one of us," the vampire said without introducing himself, "but you're not, are you?" He looked down at Trent's half-finished drink.

"I was once. I got better."

"Bullshit. There's no way … wait, over there." He gestured to a booth that had just opened up.

Once in a more private setting the vampire continued. "As I said, there's no way people like us get better. We die, we rise, we hunt, we drink. And the only way out is the stake, the blade or the flame."

"The stake is no way out," Trent told him, "it's worse than the sun. But there is another way."

Trent told him how drinking consecrated wine had driven the craving for any lesser vintage from him.

"And you don't feel it?" the other man asked, looking at the crowd in the bar, drinking, dancing, having a great time and all unaware of the hunters in their midst. "You don't feel the pulse of everyone in this room calling to you? Tell me that right now you don't feel the same urge I feel, to pick one cow from this herd and drain her dry."

Trent smiled. "I feel the urge; I hear the call of blood. But I don't want it and I don't need it. Not when there's something stronger and sweeter waiting for me every morning at Mass. It saved me; it can save you if you're willing to believe."

The vampire put his hand on Trent's shoulder. "I believe you, friend. I believe that you wanted out and found a way that works. And I believe it works. It makes sense now that I think about it."

As quickly as Trent's hopes rose at the man's words they fell again when he said, "But I think not. I like my life, or whatever you'd call it. Sure it was rough at first, but now, well, look at me. I wasn't much of a hit with the ladies when I was alive. Now watch."

The vampire looked over the crowd until he met the eyes of a young girl. Without a word she left her friends and started walking towards him. As she did he broke contact, releasing her from his compulsion, leaving her dazed in the middle of the room.

"See that? That bitch would have done anything I asked, here and now, back at her place or anywhere I wanted. Not bad for bald, fat and fifty. Use 'em, abuse 'em, tap 'em for pint and lose 'em. So I ask you, friend, why should I give that up?"

"For your immortal soul?" Trent's reply was sincere, with no trace of humor or irony. Still the man thought this was very funny.

"Friend," he said when he had finished laughing, "to be forgiven you have to be sorry and let me tell you, I ain't done a single thing I regret. Now for some reason I like you and since you're not the competition I thought you were when I first came in, there's no cause for us to fight. So let me give you a bit of advice."

The vampire's smile was not one of friendship or joy but one of warning, a feral grin that revealed his deadly canines.

"Go preach somewhere else. Leave this city and I mean soon. I catch you around here again, you come between me and my prey, well, let's just say I'll be tasting that Jesus-juice second hand, if you catch my drift."

With nothing else to say, Trent got up to leave. The vampire had one last comment. "I'd wish you luck, but I don't think you'll have any."

The vampire was right. Trent saved no one. The others he found either refused to believe that they could be saved or, like the first, laughed at the idea that they would want to be. They were damned they insisted, damned to Hell and damned to enjoy what life they had until someone ended it. When he tried to explain, to tell them of the only Blood they needed, they each rejected him in their own way. Some just ignored him and others attacked him. Some would have turned him again; remade him into a creature like themselves, but their bodies rejected his blood and recoiled from the taste of it.

So beaten and bruised in body and soul but still determined to repay the debt he owed, Warren Trent returned to Baltimore to see if he could be of service there.

***

AT NIGHT, downtown Baltimore comes alive. North and east of the Inner Harbor and its many tourist attractions are bars and night spots catering to every musical taste. Bar Baltimore, Howl at the Moon and Have a Nice Day Café attract a young crowd and hold outdoor concerts every weekend, which as far as its patrons are concerned start on Thursday. A bit south on Market Place the Iguana Cantina and Baja Beach Club have their own fans. Lovers of Irish cuisine gather at the James Joyce and just on the edge of Little Italy, Rodeo's advertises that it has both kinds of music — Country *and* Western. So popular are these clubs that the streets are packed with people, brought in by cars and stretch limos and bused in from the local colleges. For most that makes downtown an all night party. For a certain few, it makes it the perfect hunting ground.

Guthrie's was a new club, located just two streets away from Baltimore's infamous Block. Its draw was a late Sixties, early Seventies theme, celebrating all those things that the parents of its patrons had lived through and by now had forgotten, or at least pretended to. Black light posters covered the walls, lava lamps were on the tables and all the drinks were named after rock and rollers who had died in plane crashes or of excessive living. The music was loud and every song played had originally been released on a 45 rpm record.

She stood out. Young by most standards, her seeming thirty years was old for this crowd. Her appearance was also more conservative. She wore a party dress of course, but its hem was a little longer and its neckline a little higher than fashion said it should be. She sat at a corner table, a Lizard King in front of her. She'd ordered the drink for its name, not knowing what was in it. It didn't matter; she had no plans to drink it.

He stood out as well. He was at most eighteen, despite whatever his fake ID said. His clothes were a season out of style and when he tried to move to the music he was always a beat out of step.

Obviously there by himself, the woman watched with amusement as he tried to mingle. He'd hang on the edge of a group hoping for an invitation to join in. Each time he was not so much ignored as simply not noticed. He twice summoned the courage to approach a girl. One looked past him as if he had suddenly disappeared and the other simply shook her head and gave him the smile normally reserved for an annoying little brother.

He was perfect.

Leaving her drink on the table, the woman walked over to the bar.

"Here alone?" Her accented voice was full of foreign adventure and exotic promise.

It took a moment for the young man to realize that someone was actually talking to him.

"Is it that obvious?"

"A bit." She him a genuine smile, as if she were truly glad to be with him. And in her way she was. "I am Sandhya."

"That's a beautiful name."

"Thank you, it's Indian for evening. And you are...?"

He shrugged, "My name's Dale. I'm afraid it doesn't mean anything."

He may have been socially inept but Dale was not a stupid person. He knew Sandhya wanted something and during the awkward pause in the conversation he wondered what it was. He knew what he hoped it would be, such hope fueled by years of covertly reading the letters in his dad's *Penthouse* magazines. But they were fantasy and this was real life, so what she probably wanted was a ...

"Buy a girl a drink?"

Yeah, that was it. What the hell, it beat sitting alone, and she wasn't bad to look at. At least she'd help him generate some fantasies of his own.

"Sure, why not. What are you drinking?"

He ordered Sandhya another Lizard King and got a replacement for his own hardly touched Natty Boh, once a Baltimore brew and now made somewhere else.

Putting her glass to lips that barely touched the drink it held, Sandhya looked Dale over. So young and eager, full of unspent energies and unfulfilled desires, he was just what she needed.

Putting her drink aside, Sandhya made a show of scanning the room. Then she turned back to Dale. "It seems neither one of us quite fits in here. Maybe we should go somewhere else?"

"Such as?"

"I have a room at the Harbor View. It's such a nice night, we could walk there."

Dale had class the next day, an important exam. He'd miss his bus and had no idea how he would get back to Pennsylvania. None of that mattered. All those letters he had read were suddenly coming true at once. And he had no doubt that he'd learned more from Sandhya than college could ever teach him. He nodded dumbly and muttered something unintelligible. Considering this assent, Sandhya took Dale by the hand and led him into the night.

***

IT WAS a Sunday morning when Bill Thomas snagged the body. He had been fishing behind the old BG&E plant off Russell St. when he hooked something big. When Bill started reeling it in and it didn't fight back he figured his line was caught. Then he reeled in again and whatever it was moved easy. Tire or something. That's what Bill thought until he pulled it closer.

It was clear that whoever it had been was beyond help. That didn't stop Bill from wadding into the dirty water of the Patapsco River's Middle Branch to pull the body to shore. No way was he going to leave it floating and hanging on his line until the police arrived. That just wasn't done.

Bill called the police on his cell and with nothing else to do looked over his catch of the day. The dead didn't bother him, not much anyway. He'd been to the desert war and a lifetime ago he'd been a fire fighter. It was, or had been, a woman. Young, late teens, early twenties. Her skin was fish-belly white and the crabs had been at her. Only fair, Bill thought, having worked his way through a dozen hard-shells on more than one summer night. Then he started noticing damage and injuries that went beyond anything the river and its denizens could have done. The more he looked the more he realized that he wasn't as tough as he thought. He had just finished emptying his stomach into the water when the Southern District patrol units arrived.

When the call came in for a floater in the Southern, Earl Beasley surprised his fellow detectives by jumping on it. They looked at each other, shrugged and went back to their morning coffee, donuts and the sports talk shows on cable. They figured Beasley had his own reasons for going out on a Sunday morning, ones that probably didn't include looking at a dead body. No doubt that was just an excuse.

Contrary to popular belief, Earl Beasley was not a stupid man. Nor was he a lazy one, not in his mind anyway. He just believed in working smart, not hard. His style suited him, his clearance rate was always close enough to average and he did it using good old-fashioned police work — legging it around, talking to snitches, questioning witnesses and cracking suspects.

The crime lab technician was already there and taking photographs when Beasley pulled up to the scene. Like he's going to be a big help, the detective thought. While he had to admit that the Crime Lab was useful on rare occasions, mostly all the technicians did was take pictures, swab for blood and pick up cartridge cases. It wasn't like they ever found him a fingerprint when he really needed it. And with any evidence they did find it was always, "Get us a suspect and we'll make the match."

"Hell," Beasley had said to more than one tech, "if I've already got a suspect, why do I need you."

"Maybe I'm getting old," he said to himself as he walked towards the water. "Of course you're getting old," another part of him replied, "that doesn't mean you're wrong."

The crime lab guy was Jake Lawson. "It's a bad one, Detective." Beasley ignored him and looked at the body, noting the types and positions of the wounds, holding them up against a pattern in his head, seeing if they fit. Satisfied, he stepped away.

"This is what you're going to do, Lawson. When the Medical Examiner picks up the body, you're going to follow it back to the morgue."

"We don't usually go to the M.E.'s office."

"You go wherever the hell I tell you to go, and today you're going to the morgue. When you get there, you take whatever pictures the doctor tells you to. Got it?"

"Got it."

Beasley thought about telling Lawson to bring the photos to homicide as soon as they were developed and to make sure no one but him saw them. But he knew that was the best way to make sure everyone looked at them. So he kept quiet, made like it was just another homicide and hoped no one would wonder why he was so interested in found bodies.

***

"IT'S JUST like the other two," Dr. Peter West told Beasley later that afternoon. He'd just finished the autopsy on the woman pulled from the river. "Broken neck. What looks like bite marks all over her body, each over a vein or artery. Almost total exsanguination. Welts on her wrists and ankles as if she had been chained hand and foot. When are you going to let your department know there's a serial killer loose in the city?"

Beasley shook his head. "Ain't up to me to tell them. I just file the report and work my case. They can't add two and one it's not my problem."

"I get the feeling that you'd rather they didn't figure it out."

The detective looked at M.E., then down at the ravaged body on the metal table. "This is some strange shit, Doc. And there's been lots of strange shit going on in this city for little over a year now. Women on Federal Hill raped and murdered. I was on that case then I wasn't. Next I heard it was closed out. No arrests made, no warrants issued. Just 'Closed by Special Circumstances.' Another case I was on, young kid ripped apart in her bedroom. Only her parents could have done it. Special Investigations takes it over, the parents go free and again it's 'Closed by Special Circumstances.'

"You suspect some sort of conspiracy?"

"I don't know what to suspect. But let me ask you. You remember about a year ago, someone broke in and stole a body?"

"There was no sign of a break-in but a body went missing, yes."

"The dead guy's name was Trent, and it turns out he was a suspect in a series of murders just like this one here. People attacked in the park, their throats ripped out, massive blood loss. Not exact, but close enough that when I read about the first one of these in the 24 hour report somehow I knew there'd be others. When the second one came up I swore if I could I'd grab the third."

"Why the interest? Especially when there's so little to go on. Unidentified female, killed in an unknown location. Forgive me, Detective, but from what I've heard it's not like you to take on unsolvable cases."

"Any case is solvable, Doc, if you get the breaks and you want it bad enough. This gal here won't be unidentified long. And there'll be something that links her to the others. As to why I'm interested? Those cases I told you about? Each one involved a cop named Bianca Jones. That bitch gets involved in one of your cases it ain't yours anymore. It gets closed and sealed and nobody goes to jail. It ain't right and it ain't justice."

Again Beasley looked down at the young woman. "I'm going to close this case like it's supposed to be closed. I'm going to find who killed this girl and bring him in. And if along the way I learn anything about Miss High and Mighty Bianca Jones, so much the better. This is one killer she ain't letting walk away from what's coming to him."

Doctor West filled out what forms were necessary to record the cause of death and to release the body should it be identified and family located. When he was done he thought about the detective who had just left. He'd worked with him before. Never had Beasley shown so much passion about a case, or any passion for that matter. He suspected that the detective's interest lay less in finding justice for the deceased than in his dislike for Bianca Jones. Speaking of whom, the doctor remembered, the memo from the Chief Medical Examiner was quite clear. He had a phone call to make.

***

"THIS IS Dr. West of the Medical Examiner's Office calling for Detective Jones. I'm calling in reference to unknown female 132. Our Chief has directed us to contact your office in the event of any 'unusual' death.

This certainly qualifies. I'm faxing my report to you but here are the details."

Bianca Jones listened to her answering machine as the voice of Dr. West described the results of his autopsy. When he got to "if you need any more information please feel ..." she stopped the message and played it back.

"Damn," she whispered softly as West's voice came on. "Damn," a little louder as he detailed the damage done to the woman. "Damn," louder still when he gave her reference numbers for two similar deaths. And a final "Damn," this time almost to herself, as the message ended.

So much for redemption, she thought, remembering a priest's words from a year back. At least this time it was an enemy she knew how to take down. She picked up the phone and called her boss.

***

"TRENT'S BACK."

So that's what was troubling her, Joe thought as he held Bianca in his arms. He had sensed there was something wrong. Normally she allowed him to take the lead in their lovemaking — side by side, him on top, her on top, slow and easy, hard and fast. At times she even surrendered to him totally, hardly moving at all, allowing him to do whatever he liked to satisfy them both.

"I try to control things too much," she explained to him one night. "It's good to give that up at times and you're the only person I can trust."

Tonight had been different. Bianca had taken command from the start. Before they even undressed she forced him to the bed. Getting on top, she stripped off just enough of their clothes to mount him and ride them both to a fast climax. Later, naked and under the covers, him on top this time, she still set the pace and rhythm, her body demanding that he please her before allowing him his own release.

Afterwards she held him tight. And just as he was about to drop into a lover's sleep she told him.

"Trent's back."

Those two words said it all. It wasn't just that a killer who'd gone free had returned to kill again. It was a feeling of helplessness and failure. A once resolved situation had suddenly come back to bite them and people were dead who would be alive if the job had been done right the first time.

Every cop, and most times the crime scene tech counted himself in that group, had felt it. The "what ifs" and the "should haves" start crowding around and you begin to doubt yourself and the job you're doing, start to wonder if you're making a difference.

He knew Bianca felt this more than most. Her job wasn't just to lock up the bad guys. Hers was to stand firm against pure evil, to keep the Darkness away from those she'd sworn to protect.

His job was to be there for her, to help her fight her own demons.

"Joe, there's a monster inside me," she told him one day. Their friendship was growing towards intimacy and she wanted him to know.

"I'm told there's one in all of us."

"No, I mean a real monster." She told him how in a dream state she had fought a nightmare that had killed one girl and was threatening others. To stop it she took it inside herself. And it was there still, a part of her now, wanting to break free, waiting for her to release it.

If she thought he'd turn away from her she was wrong. He knew then that while it was her job to protect the city, it was now his to keep her safe as only a friend and lover could. He held her and told her of his love.

Now the vampire was back. Another monster she'd fought and contained; only this one got away. No wonder she'd been so aggressive tonight. She'd needed to be in control of something.

"Did you hear me, I said ..."

"Yes, I heard," he replied gently. "How do you know?"

Bianca sat up, the sheet falling to her waist. Distracted as always by the sight of her bare breasts, Joe still managed to listen to her tell about the young woman recovered from the water and the two others like her.

Gradually the mood in the room changed. Lovers still, but now they were colleagues discussing a case.

"I thought you were supposed to be notified of any potential serial killings or bizarre killings."

"So did I. Put it down to the first two murders happening on two different shifts and those jokers in Homicide not talking to each other. The only reason I found out is the memo the Chief sent to the Medical Examiner's."

"What do we do now?"

"The usual. Chief Williams is getting copies of all the reports. You're already detailed to work the forensics and a description of Trent is being put out to the districts."

"What about Beasley?"

"Like always, Joe. Let him work his murder. You never know, he might get lucky."

The pair settled in. As the lights were turned off Joe asked, "What if it isn't Trent? What if it's another vampire instead?"

"That's your job. Run the tests; prove it one way or the other. Trent or not, I'll have a sharp stake ready. No mercy this time, Joe. No shot at redemption. This time the bloodsucker pays."

***

THEY hadn't been in the hotel room long. Dale had watched in wonder as, unashamed of her body, Sandhya undressed slowly, giving him his first look at a naked woman not on a DVD or computer screen. At her gesture, he stripped off his own clothes and joined her on the bed, thanking God for the opportunity and praying that he would not finish too quickly.

She fell on him, taking his hard member in her hand and stroking it with a touch both firm and gentle. As she did, he let his hands roam over her body, enjoying the smoothness of her skin. Then her lips were on his neck.

Pain mingled with delight as his senses were flooded. Dale felt himself come but that was only the least of his sensations. His body was on fire as Sandhya sucked and lapped at his neck. She shuddered against him and he knew no more.

He woke up chained to a bed, naked, hands cuffed to the headboard and ankles bound to the foot posts by heavy metal shackles. No longer in the hotel room, he was, judging from the cinder block walls and high curtained windows, in the basement of a house. His screams went unanswered but that didn't stop him from crying for help until his throat was raw. Exhausted, he felt himself falling back into unconsciousness. His last thoughts were that his mother had been right about strange women in bars.

She came to him the next day, the strange woman who called herself Sandhya. By then Dale was past being scared. He was tired, weak from hunger and sore where he had rubbed his wrists and ankles raw and bloody trying to escape. He had soiled himself several times, his bowels and bladder both betraying him despite his efforts to hold back. He was crazed and desperate and he smelled bad.

When Sandhya appeared in his line of sight Dale thought that one way or the other it was over. She'd kill him or set him free. He didn't care which. All he wanted was an explanation of why she had done this and why she had chosen him.

Sandhya came close, seemingly not bothered by the stench of his body. She unlocked the cuff on his left hand and Dale had a vision being set free, thrown into the street naked and dirty and trying to explain his condition to a passing cop. Right then it was the one thing he wanted most in the world.

Release was not to be, nor was explanation. Holding him firmly by the wrist, Sandhya looked at her prisoner with equal parts pity and disdain. Then she studied his arms for a few moments. Finding a spot she liked, Sandhya bit deep into a vein.

Again Dale's body betrayed him. Against his will he felt himself get hard as unwanted pleasure raced through him. It shouldn't feel good, being used like this, but he couldn't help it. He groaned in misery even as he ejaculated in climax.

Her need satisfied, Sandhya left the boy without a word, making sure to secure his arm back to the bed. This one, she decided, would last a week, maybe more before succumbing to hunger, thirst and blood loss. She used to feed them, those that would eat, before realizing, starving or not, their blood tasted the same. If anything, her victims' lack and longing for food and drink only sweetened her feeding.

This one makes four, she thought, watching as her captive dropped into troubled sleep. Maybe one more, she thought. By now her leftovers had probably been found. Eventually the authorities would connect at least some of her victims. It was time to make plans to leave the city. Shame, she thought, Baltimore is such a nice, friendly city, so full of life.

Leaving the boy, Sandhya climbed the stairs to the first floor and locked the basement door behind her. With no need that night to see or be seen, Sandhya decided to stay in a watch a movie. Which one, she wondered, Lugosi or Lee? She settled on Langella, that one was always good for a laugh or two.

***

JOE HAD brought the results of his forensic examinations to Bianca's office along with a morning cup of coffee.

"What have you got?" she asked hoping for the short version. No such luck. Joe was in full Crime Lab Guy mode so Bianca sat back, sipped her coffee and let her boyfriend show off.

"In comparing the two sets of victims, I first discounted the differing methods of attack between the first group and the current ones. As Morgan said, a year ago Trent was just getting started; he may have learned better table manners. Next I sent casts of the teeth marks on the current victims to a forensic odontologist at the University Dental School. Her conclusion — human, all from the same set of teeth. Which doesn't help us much. Last year's victim's had their throats torn out. No teeth marks are available."

"And because of that there's probably no suspect DNA from Trent's known victims. The flow of blood from the wounds would have washed it away."

"Something like that."

From Joe's smile Bianca could tell that she'd missed something. No matter. She'd play Watson for now.

"But this time around the M.E. did take swabs from the bite marks on our victims. The last one, the girl from the water, nothing. But there was enough material from the first two for a DNA profile."

"Which does us no good because we don't have Trent's DNA. Nothing from his victims. And he walked out of the morgue before they could collect any kind of a sample. There's nothing to compare."

"Not officially."

"What have you got, Joe?"

"That stake you rammed through Trent's heart? Before we tossed it I swabbed off some of his blood. Buried it in Evidence Control in your name under a phony complaint number."

"I could just kiss you."

"You better wait. I did the comparison. No match. It's not Trent."

There was no reason that this news should have been welcome. People in her city were still dying, being killed by a blood-sucking monster that was her responsibility to hunt down and destroy. Still a sudden sense of relief washed over Bianca as the weight of failure lifted. Sparing Trent had been the right thing to do. Now that they were no longer playing catch-up, it was a whole new game.

"You still get that kiss."

"Then let me try for double or nothing. I ran further genetic tests on what sample was left, looking for certain genetic markers. The vampire's DNA has two X-chromosomes. Our killer's a woman."

***

THE KILLER might be a woman. This thought did not

surprise Earl Beasley as much as it would have last week, before he identified the victim fished from the Patapsco and learned that she was a lesbian. That's gonna be fun, he thought, checking out all the dyke bars in the city. Then he made a mental note to use more acceptable terminology when he made his report to the new Homicide chief.

Pompey Fredericks, two hundred and fifty pounds of angry black woman and all of it mean. No, to be fair Beasley had to admit that while some of it was mean, mostly the new major was intense. Fredericks was hired when the BPD was mostly white and male. She had had it rough and the fact that she was a "two-fer" didn't help her situation any. Or maybe it did. Maybe it made her work harder and smarter than anyone else in her recruit class. And if she made sergeant for reasons other than merit, from what Beasley heard that didn't stop Fredericks from being damn good at her job. Slowly she worked her way through the ranks, seemingly gaining another twenty-five or thirty pounds with every promotion.

Her latest assignment was the most difficult. She'd been brought in to replace a popular but ineffective Homicide Chief who left the unit with its lowest clearance rate in over a decade. Having had to work to a standard just slightly above perfection all her career, Fredericks accepted no lesser effort from the men and women under her command. She had made that clear at her first full staff meeting.

Detectives, sergeants and lieutenants from all three shifts, all were gathered in the Homicide roll call room. Early arrivals found a place to sit, latecomers stood wherever there was room. Fredericks had detached the Board from its usual place on the squad room wall and was standing in front of it.

The Board was the indicator of how well the unit was doing, a study in black and red of the year's homicides. Names in black were closed cases, those in red still open. At that time the Board was awash in crimson.

Fredericks waited until the room quieted on its own before starting. As murmured conversations died down to isolated whispers, she looked the members of her unit over one by one, catching the eye of as many as she could. Sure that she had their attention, she began.

"It is said that we work for God. There are signs to that effect on the desks of many in this room. Well, if that is true ..." she turned and looked at the Board, "... then God must be plenty pissed at the work we've been doing. This ..." Fredericks slapped at the Board "...is bullshit and will no longer be tolerated." She dropped her bomb. "At the end of the year, the three investigators with the lowest clearance rates will be transferred back to patrol. The sergeant whose shift has the lowest collective clearance will join them and lieutenants, you better pray that all four of these soon to be former detectives do not come from your squad or you will be the new night shift boss in the district furthest from your home. Any questions?"

They all had them, but no one dared to ask, no one except...

"Chief?"

"Yes, Beasley?" He wasn't surprised that she already knew his name.

"Is that the whole year's clearance rate or just starting from now?" It was a dumb question but the best he could do. He didn't like to be bullied or threatened and he thought maybe he should show this woman that not everyone was afraid of her.

Fredericks looked at him then turned and looked again at the Board. "These victims all demand justice. Not one of them should be dismissed. If you think they should, Detective, then maybe you should be as well. Any other questions?"

There were none, and the meeting ended.

And from that day on, Beasley remembered as he looked over the folder of his latest case, of all the people Madame Pompey doesn't like, she doesn't like me just a little bit more.

It was with this thought that Detective Beasley walked into Major Fredericks's office with perhaps one of the dumbest ideas he'd ever had, one he was hoping to scam her into going along with.

"Major, you got a minute?"

"Is this important, Detective?"

"Yes, Ma'am, I think it is."

He then told Major Fredericks about the three bodies — the case he caught and the other two, a man in Leakin Park and another one fished from the Lake Montebello reservoir. All three with broken necks, all with similar injuries and massive blood loss.

"And what is your point, Detective? That there is

another serial killer loose in the city? You know the procedure. Coordinate with the detectives working the other two cases and close the cases before some-one else dies or before that woman from Channel 11 finds out."

"Well, Major, I went looking through the files and found other cases that might be linked. Last year, before you took command, there were some killings in Druid Hill Park. And before that, a bunch of rape-murders on Federal Hill."

"Detective, it may surprise you but I'm not alto-gether ignorant of what went on before I took com-mand of this unit. I read up on those cases and I fail to see how they're connected to the current ones."

"They're not." At Fredericks's surprise, Beasley went on. "Those past cases were dumped, or rather, reassigned to Special Investigations. Actually, SI took them away from us. I thought maybe that since those guys seem to like the freaky cases we could make them a present of these."

"So you're suggesting that we abandon our respon-sibility to three dead people and hand it over to a unit whose investigative method is to look then declare the case 'closed by special circumstances.'"

Beasley tried to look both embarrassed and shifty, as if trying to inveigle the Major into an underhanded scheme. "Well, Major, however they're closed the cases do come off the Board."

Fredericks looked at him with undisguised con-tempt. This was how she usually looked at him but now Beasley had given her a reason.

"I thought it was something like that, Detective, and frankly, I'm ashamed that an officer under my command could think that way. No, actually I'm sure that many of you think that way; it's just that only you would have the balls to say it out loud. Which doesn't really surprise me. Here's what I'm going to do. The first two cases — Montebello and Leakin Park — they are coming off their position on the Board and going under your name." Here Beasley felt he ought to protest and so he tried, but, as expected, Fredericks cut him before he could say a word. "You are now off rotation and the primary on all three cases. I expect daily reports, progress within the week and a satisfactory solution in a month. You have all the resources of the department behind you. Close the case or pack up."

"Major, this isn't fair. I was only trying to help."

"You were trying to help yourself out of work, Beasley. Instead you're in the jackpot. And for that I thank you. Dismissed."

Beasley watched with open disgust and disguised glee as the names of two more victims went up in red under his own. He wasn't worried about changing them to black. With all three identified, how hard could it be to find a common link?

***

IT WAS chance, or maybe fate that took Trent to Rodeo's. He was there looking for nothing more than a pleasant evening. Good food, decent music and a chance to be around people again. He'd been alone for so long, keeping himself apart from everyone in his failed quest to redeem the earthbound damned. Now that part of his life was over and it was time to find a new path. It was time to be human again.

The band was doing a halfway decent version of "The Devil Went Down to Georgia" when he felt it, the same feeling he'd had in Philadelphia, Pittsburgh, Chicago and the other cities where he'd encountered the undead. He looked toward the entrance.

Wearing a flannel shirt and custom fit jeans she looked, despite her foreign features, every bit the country girl. Trent recognized her at once as the creature who had set him on the long road to Hell. Somehow he knew that telling her of the healing power of the Blood would be time wasted, that there was no good in her, that she would most likely seek to reclaim what she might view as hers. Trent started to ease along the walls, hoping to leave without being noticed.

Sandhya walked into the cowboy bar and looked over the crowd, wondering if it would make a good hunting ground. The boy was almost used up, good for one more feeding before he had to be discarded. She'd leave the body in the basement. Her lease was paid for another six months so it would be a while before he would be found. By then she would have drunk deeply one last time and moved on. Her arrangements were almost complete.

Suddenly a scent, a feeling, a tingle in her spine, Sandhya knew that she was not the only hunter in the room. She extended her senses, seeking him or her out. She caught the merest trace of someone familiar just as he left the bar. Of course, she thought, recognizing her own as a mother would her child. She wondered if they'd meet again and if so would there be conflict or incest, or maybe a bit of both.

Trent stood in the shadows and watched the door of Rodeo's. If she was here then people were dying. This must be why he had felt compelled to return to Baltimore, to somehow stop her. He'd wait and watch from a distance, beyond the point from which he could sense her presence. She would be blind to him as well and he could follow her home.

And then what? He knew from past experience he was not a physical match for a vampire. Then he remembered the names of those who had saved him — Bianca Jones, Joe Russo, a priest named Lawrence and someone called Morgan. Jones and Russo were both with the police he recalled. Jones had been very much interested in having him pay for his crimes. Well, so was he. Trent decided he'd track the woman to her lair then make a few calls.

***

COMSTAT is the daily meeting of the BPD command staff during which investigations are updated, problems are discussed, blame is apportioned and praise is given out. The latter rarely happens. Chester Williams always attends but seldom speaks up. As the major in charge of Special Investigations his business was his and his alone. He listened intently as Major Fredericks reported on the progress of the current open homicide investigations. When she finished she did not return to her usual seat but came over and sat beside him.

"You were right," she whispered to Williams as the commander of the Southeast District tried to explain an unusual rise in burglaries and home invasions in his area. "Beasley tried to dump the murders on your unit."

"Fine, let him keep thinking he's the only one working it. He can do the legwork, my people will explore the more ah, esoteric, aspects and make things ready for when the killer is caught."

"By 'your people' you mean that little girl you got working for you?"

"That 'little girl' has seen and done things that would melt the skin from your bones, Freddie."

"That would take some doing, Chet. Just the same, you watch her. If half the things I've heard about her are true, she's one scary cop, and one of these days something she does is going come back and bite her in the ass."

Williams laughed, getting a nasty look from the Deputy Commissioner running the meeting. The major nodded an apology then whispered back to Fredericks, "Don't worry about Jones. She knows how to bite back. Just make sure to send me copies of Beasley's daily reports."

***

EARL BEASLEY'S break came faster than he thought. When he searched the apartment of the woman from the river, he found a wristband from some place called "Gabrielle's." A little research told him that that was the name of the newest and hottest nightspot frequented by women who prefer their own sex. Armed with the victim's photo he went there that same night, wondering just how many supervisor's complaints his visit was going to generate.

The music didn't really stop when Beasley walked into the bar and not every woman in the place turned to stare directly at him. It just seemed that way.

"Can I help you, detective?" the young woman behind the counter asked in a surprisingly, to Beasley at least, sweet voice.

"What makes you think I look like a cop?"

"What makes you think you don't? If this is another complaint from that Young Republican club down the street ..."

"It's a murder investigation." Beasley held up the photo. "You ever see this woman before?"

The bartender took time to study the picture. "I don't know her name, but I think she was in here a few times. A nice enough body but a little too feminine for my tastes. Never left alone as I remember."

"And do you remember who she left with?"

Shaking her head, the bartender said, "A different one every time. No, wait, the last time it was with a real hot number, Greek or Spanish or maybe Indian."

"Dot or feathers?" The question slipped out before Beasley could stop himself. Here it comes, he thought.

The bartender smiled at Beasley's obvious discomfort. "Since you're working on the murder of one of us, I'm going to let that one go, detective. And she may have been Indian, not Native American."

That was a far as Beasley got at Gabrielle's. But the bartender at Guthrie's remembered "a hot Eurasian chick" being with the male victim from the park.

"She was in here a few nights ago too," this bartender remembered. "Picked up some geeky college kid. Lucky little bastard. Tried to score all night then that sweet piece drops into his lap. Thought the kid was gonna cream his jeans right then when she sat down next to him. Said her name was Sandy. His was Dave or Dale or something."

Great, Beasley thought, all I need is another body turning up. "Any idea where they went?" he asked, not expecting an answer.

"I heard her mention the Harbor View. That's where she was taking him. Lucky little geek."

No "Sandys" had been registered at the Harbor View in the past few weeks. There was however, a record of a Sandhya who had spent three nights there. May be, Beasley thought. At least he had a name, and more importantly, a credit card number.

Sandhya's card number led to a black account, a credit card with no names or addresses attached to it, save one registered to a corporation in an island country Beasley had never heard of. But there were a few other charges made to that card and one of them was to a Baltimore realtor who had rented its holder a house on Roland Ave.

"Thank you very much." As Beasley hung up the phone he looked from his desk over to the Board, imagining three names in red slowly turning to black. Then he pictured handing an arrest report to Madame Pompey and enjoying the look on her face as he told her of closing out three, no four, murders. That poor geek Dave or Dale is probably dead by now. Life is good, he thought as he made plans to hit the house. Tonight would do, just himself and a few uniforms. They'd catch this Sandhya at home and see what she knew about dead bodies.

***

FOLLOWING a trail similar to that of Beasley, Bianca Jones was also coming close to the killer. Receiving regular reports of Beasley's progress, Bianca decided to follow up on the man found in the reservoir. A hotel room rented in his name, a car with rental plates and an auto leasing company led her to a credit card on a no-name account. She had just heard from a realtor about a house on Keswick Rd. when Morgan called.

"Miss Jones," the old bookseller said, "Would it be possible for you to stop at the store tonight?"

"Morgan, unless the portals of Hells have opened up again I'm only a few steps away from putting the vampire business back in its coffin."

"I think I can save you a few of those steps. And please, bring Mr. Russo."

Bianca and Joe walked into Morgan's shop with no idea what the old bookseller wanted. Perhaps one of his contacts knew of the vampire's hiding place. The last thing they expected was to find Morgan calmly drinking tea with Warren Trent.

Bianca's hand went to her hip and her gun was almost drawn when Morgan held up his hand. "Please, Miss Jones, Mr. Trent is under my protection."

"For now, Morgan. But your guest has lives to answer for."

"If you think you can bring a dead man to trial, Detective Jones, I'll willingly surrender when all this is over. Or you can just use your gun on me. But let's stop this vampire first."

"What do you know about her, Trent?"

"I know she's killed several people in this city, Detective, and many more elsewhere. I know she's the woman who gave me this," Trent pulled back his shirt collar to show his neck. The scars from his previous curse were still faintly visible. "And I know where she is right now."

"Keswick Rd." Bianca said flatly.

Trent shook his head. "That must be her bolt hole. I've spent enough time with these creatures over the past year to know they always have a place to flee if necessary. I tracked her to a house on Roland Ave."

Bianca took a minute to consider what Trent had told her. Without a word she turned and searched Morgan's personal bookshelves. Finding what she wanted, she pulled down a heavy tome. She dropped it on the table.

"A Guttenberg Bible, one of the first off his press, right, Morgan?"

"Possibly the first, maybe the second, no later than the fifth."

"Swear on it, Trent. Swear that you're with us and

not her, that you'll do whatever it takes to bring her down. Just remember, the second your hand starts to burn I'll pull my gun and blow your head off. Morgan can bill me for cleaning your blood off his precious books."

To Bianca's surprise, Trent easily picked the heavy book off the table, kissed it and gently laid it back down. He put both his hands on top of it. "I swear by all that's holy, by all that this book represents, that I will do whatever I can to stop this monster and to make amends for my own sins.

"Satisfied, Miss Jones?"

Bianca nodded. "For now. Does your kind still need to sleep during the day?"

"They're not 'my kind' anymore, Detective, but yes, vampires, at least the kind that I was, sleep during daylight hours. It's less sleep, however, than a form of death."

"Whatever it is, we'll hit the house tomorrow just after sunrise. I'll call Greggs and have him get his Quick Response Team together."

"I'd like to come with you. I do have some experience confronting vampires."

"It's dangerous, Mr. Trent."

"That would be one way he could pay for his sins, Morgan. You're in, Trent. But just remember, there's no mercy for this one, no redemption this side of the grave. We stake her and destroy her body, if I have to burn the whole house down around us. Morgan, do you think you could convince Father Lawrence to join us? Having a priest on hand couldn't hurt and he could give us Communion before we set out."

Morgan's reply was interrupted by the ringing of Joe's cell phone. The crime scene tech stepped into a front room to take the call and came back with a worried look on his face.

"I don't think we have time to wait on a priest. That was a friend in dispatch. Detective Beasley just asked for two Northern District Units to meet him on Roland Ave."

"Damn it! Joe, call and get QRT on the way."

"No go, Bianca. There's a barricade situation in the Southern. An officer's down and a family held hostage. No way QRT's going to break off for a suspect roust. Unless you want to tell them we're raiding a vampire nest."

"Maybe I should. Maybe it's time to be a little more honest about what I do in the department. Maybe then we wouldn't have these problems."

"No, Miss Jones, you'd have an entirely different set of them. But that's a discussion for calmer times. What are you going to do now?"

"The only thing I can, Morgan. Trent and I will head for Roland Ave. Maybe this bitch will be out hunting. If so, Beasley's safe. If not, we'll do what we can to save his ass."

"I'm coming with you."

Bianca turned to Joe, saw in his eyes the desire to be with her, to stand at her side and face the same horrors she did. And she loved him for it. But he was not a warrior; this was not a fight he was trained for. And even if it was, she would not want him along. Joe

Russo was a kind, decent man and she wanted, no, she needed to keep him safe. He was one of the few good things in her life and she would not risk losing him.

"Joe, you have to stay here." She went on before he could protest. "This could easily go south. If it does, Morgan will need you to carry on with the fight."

Joe listened to what was and wasn't said and understood both. He nodded and watched Bianca leave, wishing her well and praying for her safe return.

***

It was twilight when Beasley arrived on Roland Ave. Daylight was fading and night was coming on. Two marked patrol units were waiting for him.

"What's the deal, Earl?" asked Rogers, the older of the two cops. Beasley's side partner back when the detective had been in uniform, Rogers never had the need or desire to be anything but regular police.

"House on the corner across the street, woman inside. Might be a witness, may be a suspect. You know how it goes." Rogers nodded. He knew. "Anyway, this time of day is the best to catch people at home, just home from work and not ready to go out. We'll go inside and talk to her, find out what she knows, feel her out."

The younger cop chuckled.

"What's with junior?"

"These new guys, Earl. They think everything is either funny or dirty. This is Blauer, fresh out of the Academy."

Beasley took Blauer's offered hand and answered

his "Pleased to meet you," with "Just so you know kid, I always laugh at my own jokes. So if I'm not laughing, it's not funny."

Ignoring Rogers's "Not intentionally, anyway," Beasley went on.

"Here's how it's done, kid. We go in. I talk to the dame. You two make like wallpaper. About ten minutes after I start, your partner's going to ask to use the can. That'll give him a chance to check out the upstairs. When he comes down you ask for a glass of water. That might get you into the kitchen. If you see anything you have your hand on your pepper spray when you come back. Got it?"

"Yes, sir."

Beasley looked at Rogers. "You got a nice polite kid there, Bill."

The three cops got to house just as the sun dipped below the rooftops. The smell hit them before Beasley even got a chance to knock. It was the smell of blood, waste and, most of all, death. To Beasley and Rogers it was an all too familiar odor that told them whatever plans they had had just been blown. To Blauer the odor was just foul, but he knew by looking at the others, their faces and their drawn guns, that this was a very bad thing.

"Should I call for back-up?"

Both older cops gave him the "rookie" look he'd gotten to know so well, so he decided to shut up and just follow orders.

Once in the house, they followed the stench to the basement, where they found the corpse of what had once been a young man named Dale.

"Oh Hell," muttered Beasley.

The naked body was lying in days-old waste. It was chained to a bed with its neck bent at an unnatural angle. What little blood it had left had started to settle in the buttocks and back of the legs. It had not been dead long.

"Number four," Beasley said to no one in particular then gave orders to the uniforms. "You two search the rest of the house. Kid, you come down and tell me what you find. Bill, secure the scene then call it in."

The officers left, Beasley took out his book and started making notes. I was right, he thought idly, but after looking at the tortured boy on the bed he couldn't take much pleasure from the fact. Should've been right a day sooner, he chided himself.

He heard noises upstairs. The rookie's voice muffled through two stories of floor and ceiling calling for Rogers. Feet frantically running down stairs. A more solid tread following. That would be Rogers. They found something.

Blauer came racing down the steps. "Detective, there's another body, upstairs in the middle bedroom. This one's a woman."

"Like this one?"

"No sir, she's all dressed and looks, well, like she's asleep."

Suddenly, it all came together. The condition of the victims, the bite marks, the blood loss. The jokes that were made when the bodies were found, jokes that could not have been true. The first set of murders in the park. Something a QRT man had told him about Bianca Jones and what she'd done to a body. It was not possible and Beasley refused to believe it. Still, it made sense and answered a whole hell of a lot of questions.

There was a thud overhead, that of a body falling and Beasley accepted the impossible.

"Shit," he swore and drew his gun.

"Kid, let's get out of here."

Beasley's revelation had come too late.

A woman came down the stairs behind Blauer. With a seemingly casual gesture she reached out, grabbed his head and twisted it. There was a crack and the rookie collapsed lifeless on the floor.

"The other one is upstairs in much the same condition," she said calmly as her gaze caught Beasley's. "You can hold a double funeral."

The detective knew he should do something — rush the woman, fire his pistol, run away — do anything but just stand there. But he couldn't. He was frozen, held by the woman's eyes as a rabbit in a spotlight.

She took the time to look him over. In his paralyzed condition all Beasley could do was look back. She was wearing a button down white blouse and jeans, her feet bare. No make-up that Beasley could see except for a trace of red at her lips. But other than that last disturbing fact, she seemed nothing special. Foreign and exotic, yes, if you liked that type, but Beasley had always gone for home-grown ladies.

"Congratulations, Detective. You broke the case

and found the killer. Too bad for you. And now you're going to tell me just how you did it."

He didn't want to tell her. He wanted to tell her to go to Hell, but the compulsion she'd placed on him was strong. He fought, his will against hers, and lost. And in a dirty basement between a monster who'd just killed two fellow cops and a corpse that stank of shit and death, Earl Beasley broke and he told this killer all she needed to know to escape the law the next time.

"It seems that the twenty-first century has finally caught up to me," she said when the detective had finished. "I shall have to be more cautious in the future. You've done me a service. Now I shall do one for you. Or rather, for both of us."

Sandhya walked over to the still form of the detective. Taking the pistol from his hand, she threw it on the bed next to the body. Ripping the collars of his suit coat and shirt, she exposed his neck.

"Relax, you're going to die happy." She bit deep and began to drink.

Beasley felt his life drain away. But no sooner had the woman begun than she suddenly stopped. "Your lucky day, detective." She released him and let him fall unconscious to the floor.

***

Sandhya had awakened from her sleep to sense the two men who had just left her bedroom. She followed, moving silently. One stopped in the first floor hallway, the one went to the basement to join another. Both were easily dealt with and the third told her all she needed to know. She would have drained him but as she started to feed she felt that tingle that told her one of her own kind was near. She extended her senses. It was her "child." He was not alone and not likely to be bringing flowers to "mother." Best that she leave quickly.

She dropped the cop, not even bothering to finish him off. Who would believe him in this day and time? There were still one or two tasks she had to complete before leaving Baltimore but that was what a safe house was for.

***

BIANCA turned off of Cold Spring Lane and on to Roland Ave. As she did, Trent told her, "She's there."

"How can you tell?"

"I have a sense of when someone like her is close by."

"So you're not fully human?"

Trent didn't reply. Bianca slowed as Beasley's unit and two marked patrol cars came into view. All three cars were empty. As they approached, a woman came out of the house they were interested in, got into a car and drove away.

"Damn." Bianca pulled in behind the unmarked car.

"What are you doing? She's getting away."

"And there are at least three cops in that house."

"Who are probably dead."

"We don't know that, Trent. If there's a chance, I have to know. And if not, then I have to make sure …"

"That they don't come back, become something like I was."

"Yes."

"Then I'll follow her and call when she gets to where she's going."

"We know where, Keswick Rd."

"And if she has a third place, one we don't know about?"

Time was running out, maybe it was already too late for the cops inside. Bianca couldn't afford to wait, just as she didn't dare let the vampire escape. She got out of her car, leaving the keys in the ignition.

"You have a cell?" Trent shook his head and she handed him hers. "Call the store when you find something. It's number 2 on speed dial. And Trent ..."

"What?"

"Don't be stupid or a hero. You and me, we have unfinished business."

Trent drove away without replying.

Bianca stepped into the now dark house, almost tripping over the body of Officer Rogers. That's one, she thought as the light from her flash revealed the angle of neck. It wasn't the time to care or mourn, that was for when the threat was over.

Up or down? she asked herself and let the smell lead her to the basement.

***

BEASLEY woke in darkness and knew he was in Hell. I deserve no better, he told himself. Rogers is dead, so's the rookie. And that kid on the bed. If I'd been a better cop, a stronger man, something more than a second rate detective they'd be alive and that bitch in jail.

No, jail wouldn't hold her, he realized, not the thing that she was. He thought of how she'd used him, stripped him of his will then fed on him. And I enjoyed it." He remembered growing erect as she started to drink. The memory only dragged him deeper into shame.

Sounds and odors began to intrude on his misery. His eyes adjusted to the dark. Pain shot through his head and neck and when he tried to move he found a tube running out of his arm. This wasn't Hell, it was a hospital.

"You're in City of Hope," came a voice from the shadows. A light turned on and he saw a small shape walk towards him. A child? No, it could only be one person.

"You lost a little blood," Bianca Jones said matter-of-factly. "You're getting fluids now, and they gave you a tetanus shot for the bite. They say you can leave in an hour or two."

"I failed them, Jones. I let them die. If I ..."

He stopped. If he went on tears would come and he would not cry in front of this woman. That would be the final humiliation.

"You did everything you could, Earl. There was no way you could have known."

"But you knew, didn't you?"

"Yes," Bianca said quietly, taking part of the blame on herself.

Beasley was quiet for a minute. "It was real; she

was real, wasn't she? She was, is a ..." he couldn't say the word. Bianca finished for him.

"Vampire."

"And last year, the Druid Park killer? Was that her?'

"No, it was — someone else."

Suddenly it made sense. Special Investigation, the kinds of cases Jones took over. He now knew why. He looked at her. How could she do it? Nothing but a little girl. Yet she was going after horrors he could not have imagined before this day. And all by herself if he knew the Department.

"I never knew."

"No one did, Earl. And that may be something that has to change."

"Jones, I ... what you do ..."

She knew different, but Bianca said, "Just another kind of killer." This was not the time or place to talk about her mission and what it cost her. "Speaking of which there's one still out there."

"She got away then?"

Bianca nodded. "This morning QRT and I hit a house where she might have been hiding. Came up empty. Her description's been put out city-wide and I have, well, let's say a specialist looking for her."

If Trent was still looking. She worried that he'd run off or worse, had returned to what he had been.

"Well, if you find her, when you find her, good luck taking her down."

"I won't need luck, Earl. I'll have you."

If you had told him he'd been named Commissioner Earl Beasley could not have been more surprised. "Why would you want me? Looking to get killed like Rogers and Blauer?"

"This Sandhya killed them," Bianca said, remembering the name from her investigation. "And you and I know what she is. That's gives us an edge. Next time we'll be ready for her."

"You mean like crosses?"

"Wooden stakes and silver-edged blades, crosses work if you believe."

"I don't know if I do. I know there's evil out there, but I haven't thought about God in a long time."

"You murder cops always say you work for Him, so He's got to be on your side. Look inside yourself, Earl. Find what you believe and use it. Do that, and you can spit in the Devil's eye."

Bianca left him with a promise to call if anything developed. A nurse came in to remove his IV and tell him that he was cleared to leave, that there was an officer waiting for him. And as he was driven home, Beasley thought about where he put his faith. And when the revelation came, he was surprised at how simple it was.

***

WHEN Sandhya left Roland Ave it occurred to her that if the police knew about one house they probably knew about the other. She would have to abandon them both, leave with just the traveling gear she always kept in whatever car she was using. That was that way of her kind. It was not wise to get attached to material possessions. They tied you down, made you think of home, stopped you from looking for the next hunting ground. And soon there were people at your door with pointed sticks and sharpened blades.

There was a third house, there always was. This one Sandhya had rented with cash. It was not in the best of neighborhoods. She had seen three drugs transactions and had heard nearby gunfire in her one and only visit. Still, it would do for the short time she'd be there. She'd make her final arrangements, sleep, then leave the next night. And should someone break in so much the better. She hated traveling on an empty stomach.

***

TRENT lost his sense of the woman almost at once. He drove to the Keswick Rd. address Detective Jones had given him, but knew right away she was not there. He thought about going back but did not want to return a failure — again. Thinking she might want to stay in the same area he drove around in ever increasing circles, looking for her car, waiting and wishing for the feeling that would tell him she was close-by.

The neighborhood changed for the worse. Dawn came. He pulled into an alley and slept in his car. When he woke he breakfasted at a convenience store and resumed his search.

It was noon when he found the car on 27th St. off Greenmount. No trace of the woman. It was possible that he wouldn't feel her until she woke. Using the cell phone, he called Morgan's shop with his location and passed on the message to be ready. Then he found a likely place for lunch and asked around about a foreign looking woman who may have just moved in.

***

HIS wife had called it the cop closet, the place where Beasley kept his uniforms and any equipment he didn't need at the time. It was in the spare room of his house, one of the rooms that would have been his kids' if he and the wife had had any. If they had maybe he'd of been a better man. Maybe Lena wouldn't have left him. Or maybe she'd have left him anyway and the break-up would have scarred the kids for life. Who could say?

It was on the top shelf, right where he'd left it. His nightstick, the Baltimore City espantoon, a one of a kind police weapon. By tradition, each was unique, ordered when graduation from the academy was certain but not carried until your field training officer judged you ready and worthy. Some years ago a new police commissioner decided that the sight of a uniformed officer walking down the street twirling a heavy wooden club was too intimidating. The guy was from California so what did anyone expect? Then a new mayor was elected and shortly after that, another commissioner took over, this one a real cop from New York. The new guy knew the value of tradition and realized that intimidation was the point. The nightsticks came back.

The rookie that Beasley had been ordered his from Nightstick Sam, a retired cop whose hand-carved clubs were considered near works of art, so nicely made that it was almost a shame to lay them up against the side of some joker's head. To the dismay and regret of many of Baltimore's less law abiding citizens, there were not many art lovers in the BPD.

Beasley held his nightstick loosely in his hand, the business end pointing up. He released it, letting gravity take it, holding only its leather strap. As it fell he snapped his wrist, causing it to spin in the air and return to his palm. A cop's yoyo. Beasley could always tell a rookie who'd been practicing with his stick by the bruises on his thighs, arm, and face.

Better stop before I hurt myself, he thought. He hadn't carried the stick for a long time. Tonight would be the last. He closed his cop closet and went down to his basement workshop. He had just finished what he had to do when Bianca called him and told him to stand ready.

***

SANDHYA woke from her sleep having dreamt that someone was watching her. Which was strange because she never dreamt, had not since her change decades ago. That could only mean someone was watching her and she knew who.

She looked out the front bedroom window and saw him standing in the dark shadows of the alley across the street. He was talking on a cell phone. They'd be here soon. She should leave now.

No, she was tired of running. She was the hunter not the prey, and it was not like this city's police were all that smart or formidable. Those in charge of this city no doubt had dismissed what the fat cop told, assuming he'd been found. In spite of all the evidence, like all the rest they still refused to believe in her kind. That was their weakness and her strength. Let them come, she'd leave town well fed. But first ...

Sandhya left by the back way, found the men she was looking for dealing in the alley. They were wary of her at first, but she moved slowly and without threat and with the confidence of owning, like they did, a piece of the night.

"What you want?" asked the one clearly in charge. "Reefer, smack, ex — we got it all."

Sandhya shook her head. "There's a man on 29th hiding in the alley. He's diming you."

"I seen him earlier, wondered about him. So he's calling Five-0, how you know this?"

She shrugged, "Does it matter? Just thought you'd like to take care of business."

"What's it for you? Want a free taste?"

Watching the vein pulse in the dealer's neck, Sandhya thought, I'd love one, but instead she said, "Just being a good neighbor. You know we all have to get along."

The dealer gave her a nod in thanks, then another nod to three of his boys, who went off into the night. Back at home, Sandhya watched from her window as the young man whose name she never did learn was led back into the alley. She wondered if this death would be any better than his last. She hoped not. Turning from the window, she got ready to receive visitors.

***

From his place in the alley Warren Trent saw the man cross the street and come his way. He turned to find two more behind him. He knew it was useless to fight. He wouldn't have a chance and the end would only be that much more painful. He let himself be led into the shadows and hoped they'd make it quick. As he felt the blade of the knife slide into him he silently prayed for the miracle of forgiveness.

***

"I know you're the expert and all that, but isn't hunting vampires after sunset kind of stupid?"

In the car a block away from Warren Trent's stated location, waiting for his call, Bianca could not help but agree, but "… it's not like we have a choice, Earl. My contact won't know exactly where she is until then."

"Just who is your contact? Another spook chaser? Or is he another one of the undead?"

Never lie to your partner. A good rule that Bianca tried to follow. "He used to be, but he got better."

"You'll have to explain that one to me later."

"If I can. Speaking of better, how you doing?"

"Holding it in, little girl, holding it in. What happened in that basement is gonna be with me a long time, but it's something I'll have to deal with later. Right now there's a job to do and payback to get."

"Little girl." Having stopped growing at five feet, Bianca had been called that all her life. She had never liked it and usually tore whoever said it a new one. The first time they met on a scene — Bianca new in patrol, Beasley a veteran about to make detective — he had called her that. She was going to file harassment charges until her sergeant talked her out it. This time, however, there was no malice in what Earl had said, maybe even some acceptance. She let it go.

"You remember the plan?"

"Yes, but I still think it would be a better idea to send QRT in to kill anything that moves."

"And if she has someone with her, another victim maybe? We'll stick with Plan A. You and me. We go in and take the bitch down."

"And if we don't?"

"Greggs has his orders." They were the same ones she'd given him in the park a year ago and on Keswick Rd. the day before. Wait for their entry. Use lethal force to take down anyone but them who came out of the house. If there's no word after thirty minutes, go in hard, fast and deadly.

Beasley's phone rang. He handed it to Bianca. Recognizing her own number she opened it and got an address from Trent. "Thanks, we'll take it from here." To Beasley she said, "It's show time."

***

STANDING at the window, Sandhya watched the lone figure approach her house. She seldom laughed aloud, but this time she couldn't help it when she recognized the fat cop from Roland Ave. He must have liked it, some of them do. No, she decided, this one is here for revenge and comes alone to redeem his honor. Still laughing, Sandhya thanked the God she had long ago abandoned for the macho American male.

Wondering just what she was going to do him, Sandhya let the detective enter before meeting his eyes. This time, however, things were different. This time she found no weakness, no fear, only confidence and determination. This time he would not break.

No matter, Sandhya did not need to bend his mind to kill his body. She advanced on him anxious for another taste of his blood.

As the woman came for him, Beasley extended his arm, showed her what he held in his hand. She pulled back, expecting a cross. When she saw what it really was, a shield of polished metal, she smiled, and tried to move towards him, only to be held fast by Beasley's detective badge, the symbol of all he held holy — the power of the Law and his belief in it.

The look of surprise on the woman's face at what Beasley did next was almost worth his ordeal in the basement. With a solemnity he had never before given it, Beasley began to recite the warning.

"You are under arrest for murder. You have the right to remain silent. If you give up that right …"

He can't be serious, Sandhya thought. He can't mean to arrest me. Held by the man's belief, she looked deep into his eyes and saw that this man was indeed very serious, that he meant every word he was saying. Very well, she'd let him have his moment. But just let him try to bind my wrists. And he can't hold that badge up forever.

"When he's done, bitch, you're mine."

The voice behind her broke the spell. Sandhya turned to see what appeared to be a young girl. On second glance she realized that she faced a merely mortal woman, one who stood against her in challenge, hands empty, no weapons, no holy talismans.

Easy prey, but then Sandhya looked into the woman's eyes and past them into her soul. There she found something monstrous, a power deadly and primeval, something that yearned to be unleashed, that would revel in the destruction its freedom would bring. The cop behind her could wait; Sandhya would have to kill this one quick.

Then the sharpened point of Beasley's nightstick rammed through her back.

"No!" she shouted in her mind if not aloud. "Not like this!" Her cry became a shriek of pain and she tried to move forward and off the stake, only to be pushed back by the surprisingly strong arms of the woman in front of her.

They stood there forever, yet only a few minutes went by. With Bianca holding the woman in place, Beasley pushed hard, then harder still until his stick pierced her heart and came out her chest.

"It's done," Bianca said, seeing what life there was in the vampire's eyes go out. She released her hold and let the creature fall to the floor.

"So she's dead?"

"Not yet." Bianca knew she should explain, but first she had to call off QRT. She went to the doorway and waved. Sergeant Greggs to come over.

"Any problems, Detective?"

"Another false alarm, Sergeant."

Gregg's looked down at Bianca's bloodstained slacks. "Whatever you say, Ma'am., whatever you say." Then he left to release his men, who had secured the entire neighborhood two minutes after Beasley had entered from the front and Bianca from the rear.

Beasley had watched the exchange between Bianca and the QRT commander. "That man knows more than he's saying. Maybe you should let him in on the secret."

"Maybe I should let a lot more people in on it. But that's for later." Bianca pointed to the lifeless shape on the floor. "Right now we have to deal with this thing."

"And how do we do that?"

"You're not going to like it, Earl."

Beasley thought about the nice safe world he used to live in only a few days ago, one filled with just human monsters. He remembered his ordeal in the basement, and realized that what he had done this night would not banish the nightmare but only add to it.

"I don't like anything about this mess."

"None of us do, Earl, and it only gets worse."

Using Beasley's cell, Bianca called Joe to tell him it was over and that he should bring the van. Then she used it to call her own phone and worried when there was no answer.

Joe's van pulled up. "Just heard on the radio, Bianca, a body was found in the alley over there. White male, stabbed to death."

Without having to be told, Bianca knew who it was

and said a quick prayer for the soul of Warren Trent.

***

In Western Maryland, just past Frostburg but before one comes to Deep Creek Lake, there is an estate owned by the Catholic Church. It is one of only two in North America, the other being in Nevada. No retreats are held there, and Sunday Mass is seldom celebrated. It is not usually a place for reflection or celebration.

In the early evening hours five people stood in a clearing. Father Anton Lawrence led them in prayer. "Amen," Bianca and Joe answered together. "Amen," echoed Beasley a few seconds later. Morgan, who had had to get a special dispensation from the Archbishop before Father Lawrence would allow him on the grounds, remained silent.

The five were gathered around a woman bound to a post. Chains held her tight. A stake, once a BPD-approved espantoon, pierced her back to front. She stood on a pile of wood that smelled strongly of gas and kerosene.

The priest nodded. Beasley stepped behind the woman and took hold of his stick. He pulled it out quickly.

Sandhya woke from Hell. There had been nothing — no thought, no feeling except for pain, and that had been everlasting. She swore to offer her rescuer whatever he asked, right before she fed on him.

She noticed the odor first, the smell of fuel on a pyre. Then she felt her bonds, chains of iron threaded with silver. Her sight and hearing were the last to return and as they did she heard the words of The Signing and saw a priest describe a cross in the air.

She flinched; despite the tortures she had just suffered the holy gestures still pained her. She then stood as straight as possible and waited for the inevitable.

Approaching the prisoner with the others behind him, Father Lawrence began an ages old ritual.

"You who are called Sandhya, you have committed grievous and unholy acts against man and God. Still, the Mercy of our Savior extends even to you. Having tasted the oblivion of Hell, will you now repent to save your soul and spare yourself eternal torment?"

Sandhya's reply was a terse, two-word epithet to which she added, "and your God as well."

Father Lawrence had expected no less an answer. "Very well," he said, "having rejected God's mercy you go to face His judgment." He lit the fire.

They watched her burn, watched flesh melt and bones crumble as they stood silent witness to a terrible justice. And when it was over, when the final spark went out and the wind began to spread the ashes, Joe Russo had to ask,

"Was that necessary?"

Lawrence nodded, he'd expected the question. "From the time of our founding, we of the Holy Order have been forbidden to spill blood, anyone's blood. Fire burns clean, and as it does, we hope it purifies. There is always the chance that as the mortal flames rise up they will remind the sinner of the eternal blaze that awaits him and so perhaps in his fear he will finally turn to God. It is one last chance at salvation."

Morgan spoke up. "You know, Detective Beasley, that you cannot speak of what you witnessed."

"Yeah, I know. And that means four names in red for me. Maybe I'll save Madame Pompey the trouble and put in for a transfer. Be the nicest thing anyone ever did for her."

"Bianca could use a partner."

"Thanks, but your girl plays too rough for me."

Beasley turned to look at Bianca. "I was thinking of putting in for a slot in the Sex Offense unit. After all that's happened, I think I could do some good there. What do you think, little girl?"

"It would do you good as well, Earl."

The five retired for the night and arose with the dawn for one last ceremony. In defiance of tradition, a Mass of celebration was held, one that honored the life and final death of Warren Trent.

"This young man," Father Lawrence said during the service, "fell prey to a great evil. He committed grave sins, sins of blood. He paid for these sins with service and sacrifice. Let us pray he's found redemption."

***

THE ride back to Baltimore, Beasley driving, Morgan riding shotgun, Bianca and Joe in the back seat.

"So I guess it's over."

"It's never over, Earl," Bianca replied. "There's always another threat to be confronted, a new evil to be destroyed. The best we can hope for is to keep the darkness at bay until our time is up."

"And for our own redemption at the end."

"Amen to that, Joe, amen to that."   ◆

III.
The Best Solution

"You should have waited."

Lieutenant Tavon Greggs sat back in his chair, a tired, beaten man. He had slept little in the past week. He had been busy defending himself to his superiors, explaining how and why he had led five men to their deaths. These same superiors left it to him to deal with the questions from the slain men's families, who found it difficult to accept their loved ones' deaths. Then, too, there were the reporters, hovering like vultures around any sensational death. They smelled scandal and whitewash behind the Commissioner's statement that the men had died in a gun battle with drug dealers. Little information had trickled out of the guarded hospital wing where two of the injured men still remained. Shots had been fired on the scene, but what else had actually happened had little to do with gunplay.

"There wasn't time."

Greggs's excuse sounded lame even to him. Behind

her desk, Sergeant Bianca Jones shook her head with disapproval. "There's always time to prepare properly. From what we've encountered in the past, you should know that."

"Lives were at stake, you and Joe were out of town. I thought I could handle it on my own." Bianca's look reflected Greggs's own feeling of having been a major fool. The Lieutenant continued, trying for some understanding, some hint of absolution. "Look, it's not like this was the first time we've dealt with something like this."

"Yes, but those other times ..." Bianca didn't have to finish her sentence.

"Those other times," Greggs interrupted, "you were there. You were in charge. I was backup."

"Okay, let me get us some coffee. Then you can tell me exactly what happened. After that we can decide just what to do about it."

While he waited for Bianca to return, Lieutenant Greggs allowed himself a small bit of hope.

He remembered back to the first time he had worked with Bianca Jones. Slender, with not much of a figure, just a shade over five-foot, to most people, Greggs included, Jones looked like anything but a cop. A high school kid dressed up like one, yeah, but not a cop.

Until they worked with her.

Back then, Greggs was a sergeant with the Quick Response Team. He was ordered to respond to Druid Hill Park to assist in the search for the serial killer that had been plaguing that area. Detective Jones was in charge. That's when he found out just what kind of cop Bianca Jones was.

"We're after a real nutcase this time," Bianca had told him at the time, "the man we think has been doing the park murders. This asshole thinks he's a vampire, and he may have partly buried himself somewhere around here. That's what the dogs are for. If they find him, I'll approach him alone so as not to set him off. I should be able to handle him."

Greggs remembered looking down at the mini-cop and doubting of she could handle anything, much less a crazed suspect. Then she gave him his orders.

"If I go down," she told him," you and your men are to stop him using deadly force. Head and body shots and keep firing until he stops twitching or he's nothing but little bits of flesh."

That's when Greggs started believing all the rumors and stories he'd heard about Bianca Jones.

The extreme measures outlined by Jones were not needed. She took down the killer all by herself. Greggs later learned that the killer was a real vampire.

Since that day in the park, Bianca Jones had fought and defeated zombies, witches, dark magicians, at least one more vampire and had faced down the Devil himself. Greggs had stood with her, ready to weigh in with the firepower of his Quick Response Team if it was needed. Sometimes it was, most times it wasn't.

"She was doing all the work," the Lieutenant berated himself. "What the hell was I doing, thinking I was ready to face these things alone?"

Greggs's self-recrimination was broken by the

return of Bianca with coffee.

"You look as if you could use a few good nights' rest," she said sympathetically as she handed him his cup.

"I'll rest when this monster's caught and destroyed." He looked at her. She nodded and he began his story.

***

You and Joe were out of the country (Greggs began). Detective Steele was away at DMA training. Tammy Dolan's a good kid and a great crime scene tech, but she's a civilian. That left me as the only member of our "special team" available when the call came in from Dominic Jones at the morgue. As you know, ever since that zombie got away from him he's involved himself in any case that looks even the slightest bit strange. The other pathologists are glad to be rid of them, and they'd rather Dominic be the one to explain a posting of "Death by internal insect infestation."

Anyway, I was busy with that downtown sniper who started up just before you left. We finally caught him, but it was a couple of days before I could get to the Medical Examiner's Office.

When I got there, Dominic was working on a body that had been fished out of the river. It had been there a while and was pretty much gone. Dominic looked up from his work as I walked in.

"Where is Bianca?"

"Out of the country. Some priest who works for the Vatican needed her help. I'm all you got."

"In that case, you are late."

"Dominic, it's eight in the morning, how early should I have been here?"

"Last Tuesday, but now that you have found the time, go look in the big box. They're against the far wall."

He grabbed for some kind of cutter and bent back over the body. I decided that I had been dismissed and went to see what he was talking about.

The big box is the large freezer where the unclaimed bodies are kept. How long bodies are supposed to stay in there I don't know, but it wouldn't be the first time that Dominic had changed dates on a toe tag to keep something of interest from going to the Anatomy Board.

There were three of them. Even if Dominic hadn't told me which ones they were I would have guessed. They were the only three in there whose heads had been turned around backwards.

I walked over and examined them. None of the three appeared to have been anyone anybody would have missed. The victims were little more than skin over skeleton frames. Their appearance went beyond the ravages of hunger; they looked shrunken, reduced somehow. All were wearing the ragged clothes and multiple layers that mark the homeless the mayor keeps promising to get off of the streets. Somehow, I don't think this is what she had in mind.

I checked the tags, two "John Does" and one "Jane Doe." The heads had all been twisted around to the point where the spinal cord would have snapped at the base of the neck.

I suspected right away what was going on. Still ...

Twisted as they were, it was difficult to examine the necks for the wounds I knew would be there. Nevertheless, on each body I found what I was looking for, a straight tear just at the jugular. These three hadn't been shrunken, they'd been drained.

"Death by exsanguination, in case you weren't sure." Dominic came up behind me. "I thought the first one was just a routine exposure case, but the wound and the total lack of blood suggested that he had died of something more than cold and hunger. I called Bianca right away. Somehow I got you. Since then, these other two have come in."

"What about the necks, were they found like that?"

"Oh no, I twisted them around just in case. I do not like it when my 'clients' get up and leave. It has happened twice now and I do not want it to happen again. Besides, from the looks of things, we have one too many vampires walking the streets of Baltimore as it is."

Vampires. Dominic had said it. I know we've faced these things and worse, before, but it still seems strange to say the word and know a creature like that is real. It still sounded like something out of the movies or cheap novels.

I knew right then I was over my head. I'm not an investigator, I'm the "shoot 'em 'til they drop" guy. I thought about your old partner Beasley, but he's retired and for what I've heard, not up to fighting monsters anymore. With you, Joe and Steele out of town, that left me, Tavon Greggs, BPD Lieutenant and rookie vampire hunter, to save the day.

Like I said, I'm not an investigator, but I know the procedures. With a killer to track down, I started as soon as I could.

Looking back, I don't know how I could have done it any differently. Three people dead in a week, how could I have waited? If I had known when you'd be back, maybe, I don't know. All I knew is that I couldn't stand by and let a monster hunt in our city without trying to stop it.

The first part was easy, finding the creature. It was either was native or had come over from Europe. I went online and checked undertakers, mortuaries and casket makers for any thefts, missing bodies or any strange or unusually large orders. Then I checked to see if any shipments of coffins or large amounts of dirt had arrived just before last Tuesday.

Things went the way they should have. A freighter had brought over three boxes of dirt for a "Mr. Durant." This same Durant had these boxes shipped to an address on Wilkens Ave. No luck with the casket makers and such, but then I thought to check the cemeteries. One of them reported that a mausoleum had been broken into. The bodies had been dumped and the coffins taken.

I took a team to the place on Wilkens. It was a storage facility and Durant's unit was empty when we got there. We checked with the office but Durant had moved out without notice or a forwarding address.

I finally found him after checking with realtors

and rental agents. A Mr. Durant had rented a house down in Brooklyn. The agent was glad to get rid of it and had let it cheap. It had been on the market for years and was rather run down.

Okay, here's where I made my big mistake. If I had thought it out, I might have, might have, mind you, just watched the house and waited for you. But no, I was feeling cocky, and lucky, and wanted to get this creature before he killed anyone else. And, to be honest, I was a bit thrilled to be doing it alone, without help from you, Steele or anyone else. After all, it is my job to protect the citizens of Baltimore, and I like to think I can do it without help.

I had a vision of sitting here, in your office, drinking coffee like we are now, but instead of telling you how I got my men killed, I'd just casually mention how, while you were gone, I'd tracked down and killed a vampire.

Looking back, yeah, I should have waited, but I'd found him so easy. I thought I was dealing with a very new or very stupid vampire. Even the dimmest crook knows that you don't keep using the same name if you don't want to get caught. It didn't occur to me that this monster might not care if he was tracked down, might have wanted to be. And it didn't occur to me that he might even be laying a trap.

Dominic hadn't reported any more bodies, so I decided to go in.

I did it by the book. Your book, not the BPD's. Just after sunrise my team hit the house. We all had crosses, and holy water, and me and one or two of the others had taken Communion at an early mass. We went in, and the first thing we did was make sure that all the shades were open and sunlight was coming in all the windows.

He wasn't on either the first or second floors, so that left the basement. We used axes to chop holes in the first floor. We wanted to make sure that there was enough sunlight shining into the basement before going down there ourselves. Everything was perfect, and that's when it went to hell.

We had our stakes out and were ready to go when Thompson came flying down the steps from the second floor. He landed hard, and just from the way he laid there I could tell he was dead, and had been dead before being thrown down the stairs. The way he was twisted, both his back and neck had been broken, and we hadn't heard a thing.

I froze for a second, just a second, maybe not even that long. I'd been on the second floor and hadn't seen anything. There certainly hadn't been anything up there that could have done that to Thompson. Before I could order my men back up, he came down.

Durant didn't look like a vampire. He was dressed simply in dark trousers and a white shirt, open at the neck, as if he had been resting and we had disturbed him, which was the case. He was the smallest of all the men there, about five-five and one forty. His face, though, it had a look of confidence, of superiority. I could tell that he regarded us as no more than a moment's diversion. He was our better, and we were no threat at all.

He smiled slightly as he came down the stairs. The steps had a slight turn just before the bottom, forming a small landing. There was a window at this landing, and the morning sun was streaming through. Durant briefly lost his smile as he passed through the light beam, but otherwise it didn't seem to affect him.

By this time we all had our crosses out. We'd planned for a confrontation, just in case. We'd use the crosses to force him into a corner, then douse him with holy water. Weakened, we'd be able to stake him.

Kenny was the first man he reached. Kenny stood his ground, I'll give him that. He held that cross out in a two handed firing stance, just waiting for Durant to back off. By the time we all realized that Durant wasn't going to back off, it was too late. Durant took one look at Kenny's cross, gave a small laugh, then reached out and grabbed it.

I could smell the vampire's burning flesh as he crushed the cross. Then, as quick as thought, before Kenny could retreat, Durant reached over, grabbed Kenny and ripped off his left arm.

That started it. I would have called for a withdrawal if I could. But Durant pushed Kenny on top of Thompson, then threw his arm into our midst like an ancient challenge. Then he stood there and waited as if saying, "Come get me."

There was no stopping them, or me either, to tell the truth. Two of our own were down with the killer in front of us. Ross and Martello were the first to act. They had their holy water out and splashed him with it. Again there was that burning smell, and you could see Durant's clothing and skin smoking. He ignored it and punched Ross through the chest, caving it in. Martello he picked up and threw through the window.

O'Brien drew his weapon and emptied it into Durant. The bullets staggered him as they passed through, but that's all they did, pass through. One shot did ricochet and got Johnson in the leg, taking him out of the fight. Morgan and Patterson approached Durant, holding their stakes in front of them like short spears.

As Morgan and Patterson approached from either side, I came at him from the front. He left himself open and I threw my stake, hoping for a lucky hit, or at least to distract him and give the others a chance. He wasn't distracted and they never really had a chance. He swerved to dodge my throw, then grabbed Morgan's stake and swung him around into Patterson, knocking both men down. He then reversed the stake and used it to pin them both to the floor. O'Brien picked up the stake I had thrown and charged Durant. He came close, but Durant stepped aside at the last moment, reached out and snapped O'Brien's neck.

That left him and me. I didn't know what I could to do to stop him, but I was going to try. I took out my cross, reversed it, held it like a knife and waited for him to come.

"That just might work," he spoke for the first time. He had a middle European accent and spoke like he'd been an important man when he was alive, or he wanted everyone to think so. "Yes, that might work, if it had a point and an edge."

We stood there for a time. I didn't want to attack him, but I couldn't leave my men. The next move was his.

"You are their commander, are you not?" Durant did not wait for me to reply. "I will let you live, this time. There is an odor of sanctity about you—and him." He indicated Johnson in the corner, holding his wound and trying to keep from bleeding to death. "You both took His wafer this morning, and your blood is not now fit for drinking. Take him and go."

"Not without the others." Where I got the courage I don't know, but I gripped the cross tighter and was ready for his charge.

"Oh, them. Return an hour after sundown. I shall be gone, and you can have what is left of them. Or you can die now."

If it had just been me, I might have gone after him. Ross was still alive, dying, yes, but right then still alive. I didn't want to leave him for Durant to feed on. But there was Johnson, him I could save, and maybe Martello outside. I helped Johnson up and started to walk out when his voice stopped me.

"One other thing, Officer. Do not hunt me again. You will only lose more men, and force me to turn my attentions to the more prominent members of this city. Leave me alone, and you and they will be safe."

With that he was gone.

I got Johnson in one of the cars we had come in. Martello I found outside the window he had gone through. Even without knowing just what they were I could tell his injuries were serious. Somehow I got him in the car without doing too much more damage. I drove us all to the hospital and then pretended to be in shock until it was safe to go back for the others. They were all still there, more or less as I had left them. Ross had been drained. I had Dominic twist his neck just in case. There was no sign of Durant anywhere. I set fire to the house anyway. If he was in there, he'd be little more than ash, but the next day Dominic called and told me that two more bodies had shown up. He's still out there, Bianca, and I don't know if we can stop him.

***

GREGGS ended his narrative by draining his coffee. Without having to be asked, Bianca filled it again. Greggs took another healthy swallow and placed it on the desk.

Greggs had begun his report quite matter-of-factly, as if he were on the witness stand and was testifying against any common felon. He faltered a bit when he got to the morgue and the tracking of Durant. He was near tears and collapse as he described the brutal murders of his men. His voice stayed steady, but when he finished, his black skin was almost white.

Bianca remained silent to give the Lieutenant time to recover from the ordeal of his narrative. When the Lieutenant was at least somewhat composed, she leaned forward and granted him what absolution she could.

"You did as much, if not more, than any man could, Tavon. Had I been with you, well, it might be that the

Commissioner would be looking for a new monster hunter."

The telling of his tale, completely this time, without the omissions that he'd had to make for his official report, along with Bianca's understanding, purged Greggs of the disgust he had felt for his actions so far. The guilt was still there. It would be a long time fading and would never leave him entirely, but he was whole again, ready to rejoin her in their fight against the dark things.

Bianca looked at her watch. The time was late and soon it would be growing dark.

"You need to rest," she said to Greggs in a tone that allowed for no argument. "Go home and get some sleep. Tomorrow we'll hunt this bastard together."

From work, Bianca went to her husband's bookstore. Of the surface, Morgan's Rare Books and Collectibles was just another used bookshop in Baltimore's historic Fells Point. An alley shop on Lisbon St. it appeared from the outside to be nothing more than a one room store.

Inside, however, things were much different. There was a back room that should not be there and this room was filled to overflowing with books on magic, the occult and the supernatural.

Joe Russo had inherited the shop from Morgan, its previous owner. Morgan had died fighting an Evil out to destroy the city, and had left Joe both the shop and his collection of rare and forbidden lore.

"Another vampire, Joe," Bianca told her husband after greeting him and explaining what had happened. "This one seems mostly immune to both holy water and sunlight? He also wasn't too impressed by the cross or those wielding it. Could he be something more than the undead?"

Joe thought about this for a moment, then ...

"No, if it was something else, or from some other plane, it would not have reacted at all to the water or the cross. It's some form of vampire, but what?" For the answer he turned to his books. Somehow knowing what was contained in each one, Joe's eyes searched the shelves for one title that might help. He finally settled on Seward's *The Undead.*

There was little in the book that Joe did not already know. It did confirm, however, that in some circumstances, the undead could walk abroad in the daylight, although at some cost. Still, Seward had had only one encounter with such a beast, the rest of his volume being research conducted from behind the safety of library walls. And all of that research insisted on the power of Christian symbols.

"I guess, Joe, that Seward never thought that there might be Jewish or Moslem vampires."

"Or that vampirism might predate Christ. But no matter, we've seen that the power of the symbols lies in the faith of those who use them, not in the past beliefs of the undead."

"Yeah, but Tavon and his men put their faith in those symbols and they were slaughtered. Was their faith that weak, or could it be that Durant's faith in himself was stronger than they were?"

"It could be," Joe mused, more to himself than

Bianca, "that this creature is very old, much older than Dracula or any of the others, possibly by several hundred years. A vampire that old might just develop a tolerance for holy objects."

Bianca stood and began pacing in frustration. "So how do I fight this thing?" she asked. "Conventional weapons won't work and it's effectively immune to the ones we use on vampires."

"If you had a sword and could get close enough, you could cut off its head."

"And if I had a crossbow with wooden quarrels I could shoot it in the heart, assuming it still has one, but let's face it, Joe, this thing is probably much too fast for us. Damn it, we've kicked the Devil's ass. We should be able to come up with a solution to this problem."

Joe was quiet for a few minutes then suddenly smiled. "You know, Bianca, I think you're right. We do need a solution. And I have just the one."

                              ***

THE NEXT morning, when Greggs reported back to duty, Bianca explained Joe's plan.

"Are you sure it will work?"

Bianca shrugged. "No guarantees but it's all we've got. And let's pray that Joe's right. If he's not, then the city is at this thing's mercy and we'll be either dead or his lunch."

When the two left police HQ, Greggs was carefully holding a small glass jar containing a clear liquid. There was a cloth-wrapped double-edged sword in the back seat of their unmarked car.

"Where," Greggs asked, "did you get a sword?"

"Where else, Evidence Control. It was from that mess with the fairies that Beth was involved with."

It wasn't long before the two pulled up in front of an apparently abandoned house.

"Are you sure this is it?"

"Certain, Bianca. You don't really think I slept last night, do you? Anyway, it wasn't that hard to track it down. Durant isn't making any effort to hide from us. It's as if he wants us to come after him."

"He probably does, Tavon. It's a game to him, something to while away a small part of his eternal life."

"Then it's a good thing we've changed the rules, isn't it?"

The two got out of the car and headed for the house. Bianca holding the jar as Greggs took the sword from the back seat.

Unscrewing the jar, Bianca led the way into the house.

With sufficient light streaming in through broken windows, the pair did nothing but stand by the front door and wait in what had once been a living room. They did not have to wait long.

Bianca later told Joe that Durant appeared in less than an eye blink. One moment the two police officers were in an empty room, and the next the vampire was there, standing across from them.

"Again, Officer? You do not learn fast in this country, do you?" Durant made a show of sniffing the air. "And you have been to church again. Communion with

Him will not save you this time, or your friend."

Neither offered a reply. As arranged, Bianca approached first with the jar, closely followed by Greggs.

"Did you not tell this woman that such things as that weak tea she carries will not stop me?"

At that taunt, Bianca hurled the contents of the jar into the vampire's face. Durant waited for it, prepared to shrug it off and then turn on his attacker. Instead, he fell to the floor, screaming.

"Now!" Bianca shouted. Greggs came forward with the sword and brought it down on the monster's neck. As he swung, he caught a glimpse of the now helpless creature. Its face was being eaten away, the flesh falling off to reveal the skull beneath. Some of the liquid had missed Durant's face and was instead eating its way through his clothing and into the body beneath it. There came the smell of rotting eggs, of sulfur, of Hell itself.

Greggs paused for just a moment. This creature had claimed his city as its hunting ground, had killed without mercy. This thing had murdered his men, fed off one of them and had threatened to do the same to Greggs. It was with no small satisfaction that he let the sword fall and sever its head. Without hesitation, he brought it up again, reversed it, and, remembering how Durant had staked two of his men to the floor, thrust the sword down into the body and through Durant's heart.

The two cops stood back from the smoldering body. The sword, its point pinning Durant to the floor, stood straight, its hilt and guard forming a cross over the corpse. Truly dead, the body now began its long delayed process of decomposition.

Bianca and Greggs waited until the last of the body had rotted away. Only the skull and a few bones were left when Bianca motioned to Greggs to withdrawal the sword. She then put on heavy gloves, drew a sack out from a coat pocket and gathered up the bones.

"We'll have Dominic burn these in the cremato-rium," she said, pulling off the gloves once she had the sack tied tightly.

"You know, Bianca, I really wasn't sure it would work. I prayed that it would, but I wasn't sure until I saw his face going."

"Maybe it was your prayers that did it, Tavon."

"That, and Joe's 'solution' to our problem."

"Basic science, as he explained to me. Holy water, in addition to being blessed, is still water. It retains all the physical properties of water. And one of those properties is that you can combine it with other chemicals to make solutions of various kinds."

"Like sulfuric acid."

"Yes, like sulfuric acid. Holy water affects most vampires as if it were acid. With this monster we needed something stronger. Joe reasoned that an acid made from holy water might affect him as it would us, possibly more so."

"Thank God he was right, Bianca."

"Yeah, Tavon, thank God, and let's pray that as we fight this endless battle against dark things we'll always be led to the best solution."   ♦

John L. French is a crime scene supervisor with the Baltimore Police Department Crime Laboratory. In 1992 he began writing crime fiction, basing his stories on his experiences on the streets of what some have called one of the most dangerous cities in the country. His books include *The Devil of Harbor City*, *Souls On Fire*, *Past Sins*, *Bullets and Brimstone* and *Here There Be Monsters*. He is the editor of *Bad Cop, No Donut*, which features tales of police behaving badly.

Three Golden Age heroes confront a diabolical force in the early days of World War II

Thrills!
Suspense!
Excitement!

TO BATTLE BEYOND

The Domino Lady, The Black Bat, and Inspector Lagrasse ...
An adventure of "The Originals" by C. J. Henderson